"I know who you are, Mr. Lord, and I want to help."

He watched her for the slice of a moment, his expression stormy. "I don't need your help." This time when he turned from her he began to limp away. "Get out."

There was no confusing his dismissal. It was absolute. Through the wrinkled knit of his shirt Helen could detect power in his wide shoulders and see the coil of muscle in his arms as he supported much of his weight with the cane. Her gaze strayed down to his injured leg.

He'd been the heartthrob of millions of women with his dashing good looks and his nerve. But now he was a wounded, angry recluse who hid from everyone and everything.

Yet, as weak and scarred as he was, Damien Lord was the most marvelous man she'd ever seen. Helen pushed back that thought. A famous, sophisticated world traveler like him would never be interested in a meek, plain Midwestern girl. He'd made that depressingly clear....

Enchanted Brides

The Myth

The stately D'Amour mansion stands majestically in the countryside, its absentee owner rumored to be living in Europe. Closed for years, this mansion has a charming myth surrounding it. Legend says that the mansion is enchanted and that "an unmarried woman who sleeps within its walls on her birthday, when the moon is full, will marry the first man she sees in the morning."

To Marry a Stranger is the first in Renee Roszel's **Enchanted Brides** trilogy. Look out for Lucy's story early in 1998.

Renee Roszel can't believe her good luck: she spends her days writing about the world's most eligible, most exciting, most sensual men—and she has the power to orchestrate their every move!

She is also amazed by her good luck at having three heroes of her very own—her husband and two sons—who help directly with her research into heroic behavior.

Renee loves to hear from her fans. You may write to her at: P.O. Box 700154, Tulsa, Oklahoma 74170, U.S.A.

To Marry
a Stranger
Renee Roszel

Harlequin Books

TORONTO • NEW YORK • LONDON
AMSTERDAM • PARIS • SYDNEY • HAMBURG
STOCKHOLM • ATHENS • TOKYO • MILAN
MADRID • WARSAW • BUDAPEST • AUCKLAND

To Joan Mullen
And the kittens we rescued, together
Bless you for all you've done for
innocent critters over the years

ISBN 0-373-03470-9

TO MARRY A STRANGER

First North American Publication 1997.

Copyright © 1997 by Renee Roszel Wilson.

CHAPTER ONE

HELEN woke with a start. Unfamiliar blackness enveloped her, and she flung up her hands, protectively. Where was she? Groggy, she rubbed her eyes, trying to clear the cobwebs of sleep from her mind.

She heard an ominous wail, and leaped off the couch, lurching forward. Pain in her shin made her stumble sideways. Flailing to keep her balance, she hit something with her hand. Whatever it was, it crashed to the floor, the noise as loud as a thunderclap in her ears.

Panicking, Helen grew fully awake, recalling where she was, and why. At this instant, in the pitch-dark with wild beasts shrieking in the distance, she had an uneasy feeling that her idea to come here hadn't been very wise.

She heard the cry of a wounded beast again—or was it the groan of warped floorboards? Either way, something, or someone, was coming. How could that be? The mansion had been empty and locked up for years. Nobody was supposed to be there.

Her eyes grew more accustomed to the darkness, and she could distinguish shapes. She was in a paneled den, the furnishings shrouded in white, making the place appear to teem with ghosts. She had removed the dust cover from the velvet sofa where she'd fallen asleep, but was too frightened to replace it. After all, which was more important, her life or a little dust on a couch?

The window she'd slipped through was on the far side of the musty room. As she took a step toward it, she thought she saw a shadow pass across the room's entrance. She spun in that direction, but could distinguish nothing but a shrouded wing chair. Swallowing the lump of terror in her throat, she decided she must have been wrong, for there hadn't been any sound. Or had there? Unfortunately she couldn't be sure, since her ears were roaring with the rush of blood from her pounding heart.

Still, not long ago, she *had* heard movement. Someone or something was prowling the mansion and she didn't intend to wait around to find out what it was. Her nerve gone, she scrambled around the coffee table, leaping over the lamp she'd knocked to the floor.

As she scurried to make her escape, she berated herself for her cowardice. For once in her life she'd taken her destiny in her own hands, and now, with her objective in sight, she was chickening out. The noise might be nothing more than the settling of the old mansion. But her flight couldn't be helped, she was simply not a brave person.

The faint moonlight that seeped between the drawn curtains was her beacon, and she ran around a massive desk to reach it. What a dreamer and a fool she'd been to think that testing the D'Amour mansion myth was a good idea. Her sisters would be livid if they found out. Well, since she'd failed so miserably, this escapade would be her guilty secret. The devil himself could never drag the truth from her.

She grabbed the curtain to move it aside, but as her hand touched the brocade she was captured in a hard grasp, and yelped in shock. She found herself spun around to face—what? Before her, vague in the blackness, loomed a dusky phantom. Heavens! Had she conjured up the very devil she'd boldly vowed never to admit her folly to?

She struggled in alarm but was held fast. "Please—

please...'' Her fragile plea faded, her voice failing. Shuddering with dread, she shrank as far away as she could, though her wrist was seized in a firm grasp.

"What the hell are you doing?" the apparition growled.

"I—I..." Nothing more would come out, for her thumping heart blocked her throat. Terror-stricken, she could only gape, fearing for her life. The massive specter was obscured in shadow, but Helen thought she could see a fall of ebony hair masking part of an angular face. She had the impression of a piercing gaze and a forbidding frown. Yet, more important than what she could visibly identify, she sensed great power in her captor— and even greater anger.

Just when she thought she would faint from fright, her assailant let her go. "Get out!" The jerk of his head reiterated his command, releasing her from her terrified paralysis.

Not sure how she managed it, Helen found herself scrambling through the window and dropping onto dewy grass. As she stumbled and clambered toward the nearby wood, she was grateful she didn't have a heart attack on the weed-infested lawn. No one would have found her for a week.

The woodland path was bright, lit by a full moon. Once over her initial shock and fear, she slowed her breakneck pace, then stopped, ire swelling inside her. She sagged against a wizened oak kicking at it with her loafer. "Stupid! Stupid! Stupid!" she muttered. "Helen you're the world's prize idiot!" Pressing her cheek against the tree, she picked at the rough bark. Her legs were shaky, so she took several deep breaths to restore herself.

With the reality of what might have happened to her

sinking in, she exhaled raggedly, wiping away an errant tear. What an infantile idea that had been. She supposed if she were to be brutally honest with herself she would have to admit that she'd allowed her life's goal to muddle her thinking. For as long as she could remember, the only thing she'd ever wanted was a nice man to love her. And a big, loud, happy family. *A whole family.*

Since she could hardly remember her mother, for years she'd fantasized about having a family of her own—with a mother, a father, five or six chubby children and lots and lots of pets. Was that so much to ask?

Today was her twenty-first birthday. By her age, many women already had husbands and children. But living in the country, Helen didn't meet many men—even fewer who might be attracted to a plain, painfully shy young woman like her. So she had reasoned, since husband prospects were few and far between—considering she'd never even had a steady boyfriend—it was time she took her fate into her own adult hands! The D'Amour myth had seemed perfect for her objective. Having a husband would prove she was all grown up—even to her sisters, who couldn't seem to see her as anything but a child.

She moaned into the tree bark, aware that if Elissa and Lucy ever found out where she'd been tonight, she'd never hear the end of it. They would call it the most childish stunt they'd ever heard. And she wouldn't be able to argue that fact. It had been recklessly immature.

Downhearted, she straightened, gulped air for strength and headed home. As she walked along, she renewed her vow that her sisters would never know where she'd been tonight. When she reached the rear gate that surrounded the Victorian inn that she and her sisters were renovating, she made a second vow. She would never, *ever* go near the D'Amour mansion again. Inside its imposing flagstone walls lurked either a felon hiding from the law, a demented fiend—or the devil, himself.

She'd been lucky to escape with her life.

Helen awoke in her basement bedroom with a smile on her face. It was a beautiful day—extremely balmy weather for mid-September in Missouri. She carefully dislodged her hair from beneath her sleeping, saffron-colored cat, Thalia, receiving a drowsy mew in response.

Throwing back her covers, she danced barefoot across the secondhand hooked rug that covered the cement floor. So lighthearted she could almost fly, she dashed to a narrow slice of window set high in the wall where bright sunlight was streaming in. Twisting the latch, she pulled it open and was rewarded with a sweet, woodsy breeze that rustled her hair.

Hopping onto a footstool to get a better view of the hilly Ozark countryside, she stretched, laughing with pure joy. She'd awakened with a new realization, one she hadn't considered last night when she'd been so frightened. Stepping down from the stool, she smiled at her reflection in the mirror that hung over her scarred dresser, and did a lighthearted spin.

So what if she didn't have the figure of a supermodel? So what if she had an ordinary face and unimpressive gray eyes? Maybe her shoulder-length hair was a muddy brown color that refused to curl, even when tortured with "perm" chemicals. And, maybe she wasn't the life of every party—so timid she spent more time with animals than with people.

None of those shortcomings mattered. Not anymore. For she'd woken up today with a blinding flash of revelation. *She'd fulfilled all the requirements of the D'Amour myth*. She'd slept in the mansion under a full moon, on her birthday. She might not have slept there long, since she hadn't slipped into the place until after midnight; and when she'd gotten home it was only two o'clock in the morning. Even so, she *had* fallen asleep.

Last night after her disastrous encounter with whatever it had been, she'd tried to convince herself the myth didn't matter, that it was only an adolescent fantasy. But today, with no gloom-shrouded phantoms snarling at her, she could see the wondrous truth. She'd done everything the myth asked of her, growling devils or no growling devils.

The deed was done.

The instant she'd awakened, she'd known it as strongly as she'd ever known anything. *Today she would meet her true love!* The very first man she saw would become the gentle husband she'd always hoped for—the man who would cherish her forever.

Though her usual attire was faded, cutoff jeans and a T-shirt, she hurriedly donned her prettiest cotton sundress, a pleasant mauve print that made her eyes look more silvery than the dull color of wet cement. Humming a merry tune, she flew up the steps from the basement apartment where the sisters resided. Breezing through the staircase hallway to the reception hall, she headed for the front door, which stood ajar.

"Morning," she sang out to her eldest sister, Elissa, who'd just stepped onto the front porch to pick up the morning paper.

Elissa looked over her shoulder, her grass green eyes going wide with surprise. The eldest of the Crosby girls was always up before the sun, still dressing like the Kansas City lawyer she'd been before they'd pooled their inheritances and bought this inn. Brushing her wavy, copper penny hair from her eyes Elissa smiled with recognition. "Good morning to you, too, birthday girl." She indicated the direction of the kitchen with a nod. "Lucy's fixing your favorite—blueberry pancakes. Are you good and hungry?"

Helen could only laugh as she swept by her sister out onto the wide wooden porch. "Oh, I couldn't eat right now. I think I'll take a walk. Do you mind?"

Her sister slipped the rolled newspaper under her arm, her expression contemplative. "No problem, but—where are you off to at seven in the morning? And so dressed up?"

"This old thing?" she hedged with a shrug, hoping the action looked casual. "I just thought I'd walk off some excess energy. I'll be back soon."

Looking like a lawyer who didn't quite believe her client, Elissa's eyebrows dipped. "Well, it's your birthday. I guess you can do what you want. But be careful."

Helen smiled, even in the face of her sister's everlasting mother-henning. Not even being treated like a helpless baby could upset her this morning.

When Elissa went inside, Helen walked to the connecting veranda that extended around the side of the house, and bent to pet her dog, Cracker. The shaggy mutt had been lounging on his favorite wicker chair, but with her approach, he struggled up on his three legs, wagging his tail. "No, Cracker." She patted the cushion. "You stay here. I'll be back in a little while."

Ever since the Fourth of July two years ago when she'd found the injured dog and nursed him back to health, he'd been fiercely protective of her. But this time, she didn't want him tagging along. She couldn't have him scaring off her true love.

The salt-and-pepper mutt settled down on the paisley cushion and barked a high-pitched farewell. With an answering wave, she went down the wooden steps, her heart fluttery with anticipation. Somewhere, very nearby, her true love was waiting—*for her*.

She headed out the front gate in the picket fence, then down the tree shaded lane toward Branson, ten miles away. The morning sun was bright and welcome on her bare arms and face. She began to hum again as she half walked, half skipped along the shoulder of the asphalt road. Only a few minutes passed before she heard the sound of an engine approaching from behind. She stilled in her tracks, her heart leaping. If this was a man, *then he was her destiny*.

She swallowed, nervous about turning and looking. Was he someone she knew? Was he handsome? Witty? Of course he would be witty, since he was her fated true love. He would have to be outgoing and funny to counterbalance her severe shyness. Her chest swelled with excitement as she heard the squawk of worn brakes. He was stopping! "Oh dear heaven!" she squeaked, hardly able to catch her breath. She was about to experience the most important event in her life!

The significance of the moment paralyzed her. It took several seconds and all her effort to finally twist around to stare her destiny in the face. When she managed it, she felt a moment of confusion, hesitation, as though her eyes were deceiving her. It couldn't be...

Her smile trembled for a second, then fell away. Before her was the familiar, dented green van she saw almost daily along this rural route. On the side of the battered conveyance were the unevenly scrawled words, Boggs Farm in faded yellow paint.

"Hirk Boggs?" she breathed aloud, the calamity in her tone hardly sufficient to describe her desolation. Hirk Boggs—the local butter and egg man—was her *destiny*!

He poked his head out of the cab of his van and waved broadly, then opened his door from the outside, since the handle on the inside was long gone.

Helen was so deflated, she wasn't even able to lift a hand to return his wave, but Hirk didn't seem to take it as a slight. He unfolded his spindly frame from the seat and shambled across the deserted road, grinning a gap-toothed grin. "Howdy there, Miss Crosby," he said, his lisp from lack of front teeth making her name sound like Mi-*tth* Cro-*tth*-by. "What are ya doing out here all alone?"

In an ungainly flourish, he took off his tattered straw hat, and Helen saw the flash of aluminum foil that lined it. She'd heard Hirk was afraid aliens were trying to steal his brain, and he used aluminum foil to ward off such attempted thievery. From the glint of metal, it seemed the rumors were true.

"Miss Crosby?" he repeated in his spattery lisp. "Did your car break down? Need a lift?" His pasty white cheeks grew pink, and Helen knew he was fighting his own timidity. She swallowed, trying to cast off her distress at the idea of becoming Mrs. Hirk Boggs. He was every bit as uncomfortable with people as she. How could they ever be a couple?

She finally managed to shake her head in answer to his question. "No. No car problems—Hirk." A weak attempt to smile failed at first. In a courageous second attempt, she managed to feign a grin, though the effort was agonizing. "I was just out walking." She cleared her throat. She still sounded very depressed.

Hirk belatedly sensed her unhappiness, his smile fading. "You sad about something, Miss?" he asked. "Ol' Hirk would be glad to help you out if he can." He frowned suddenly, then plopped his protective hat back on his thinning hair, apparently realizing his unprotected brain was in mortal danger.

Her heart twisted and she had a terrible time holding on to her smile. Though Hirk was pitifully eccentric, a little slow, mentally, and twice her age, he was well-meaning and kind. He would be a gentle husband and father for their children. She stifled a shiver at the thought and shook her head. "No, I'm not sad," she lied. "It—it's just such a nice day, I…" Her voice broke and she couldn't go on. *Destiny was an unkind brute.*

His blush continued to grow and expand until it had consumed his bulbous nose. "Sure 'nuff is a nice morning, Miss." When the conversation had dwindled to a strained nothingness, he grinned bashfully. "Well, uh, guess I'd better get back on my route. Like ol' pa used to say, 'Can't fool around wastin' daylight.'"

She nodded, then shook her head, hoping she was agreeing, but her emotions were too rattled to be sure. Fidgeting from one foot to another, she echoed, "Yes, you—you mustn't waste…" He was loping away, and she didn't think he could hear her any longer, so she decided to let it go. When he slammed the door of his rattle-trap van, he waved his blunt paw. "See ya around, then," he yelled as the engine sputtered to life.

When he had chugged out of sight around a curve, Helen closed her eyes, counting to ten. She wasn't angry, but she'd discovered years ago that sometimes counting helped hold back tears as well as calm anger. And she was very near tears. Hirk Boggs was her destiny.

Her fate.

Despondent, she found herself running, fleeing that fact with all the strength in her. It wasn't until too late that she noticed the direction in which she'd fled.

She was deep into the D'Amour mansion grounds.

Winded and sick at heart, she came to a stumbling halt. Not here! ''Out of the frying pan into the fire,'' she muttered, breathless. It was one thing to be in the company of a slow-witted, gap-toothed man with a phobia of aliens, but quite another to run headlong to the hideout of a bloodthirsty nut-case. Evidently she was more disturbed by the revelation of her future bridegroom than she realized.

A peculiar noise made her suck in a startled breath. Trying to remain rational, she worked at composing herself. She was nowhere near the mansion. The massive Gothic structure could just be seen over a rise, its six chimneys reaching skyward above the surrounding oak and hickory trees.

The sound she'd heard was probably nothing—a fish jumping in the sheltered nearby pond, or something equally innocuous. Her nerves were simply raw from everything that had happened to her in the past few hours—not to mention her lack of sleep. She turned to start back toward the inn when she heard the sound again. Splashing.

She stilled, worry beginning to gnaw at her. What if an animal was in trouble? What if a duck had been wounded, or a young swan? She couldn't leave without making sure no innocent creature was suffering. Shoring up her fortitude, she inched toward a stand of mulberry and cedar trees that masked her view of the pond. Creeping through the wooded area, she came to the edge of the water and crouched amid weeds. Parting the grasses, she strained to see what was making the sound.

Pain in her lower lip made her flinch, and she realized she'd bitten down hard at what she saw. The lake didn't hold an injured duck or swan, but a man—*swimming*. Muscular shoulders and arms took him briskly across the secluded body of water. She stared, transfixed by his masculine grace, of the strength in his arms and shoulders as he cleaved the surface with powerful strokes. Yet as he swam, she noted that his kick seemed awkward, a strange inconsistency.

At the far end of the pond, some fifty feet from her, he did a sweeping turn and began to swim back. Helen was jolted anew by what she witnessed. A leather patch hid the man's left eye, and angry, red scars ran along his cheek to his ear. His wet hair, sleek and dark, like rich oil, was longer than fashion dictated, but she had a feeling this grim stranger cared little for such trivia.

New apprehension pricked along her spine as she stared at his face. Defiant drama was etched in every line. It was as though he were telling the whole world to go straight to Hades. As she watched him swim toward her, she grew more and more disturbed, yet in an odd way, more excited, too. She feared the hostility in his expression. Yet, even marred and bitter as he appeared, the man was gorgeous, and her throat closed with feminine appreciation.

It hit her like a rock in the pit of her stomach, that this was the phantom she'd encountered last night in the mansion. As he approached, his muscles glistening hard and distinct in the sunshine, she unconsciously licked her lips. This was no conjured devil, but a flesh and blood mortal. She frowned, wondering why he was skulking around in the deserted D'Amour mansion like a criminal.

Good heavens! *He probably was a criminal!*

An inner voice reminded her, rather ironically, that he might say the same thing about her, since she'd broken into the place, herself. So, the question remained—was he a criminal or wasn't he? She chewed her lower lip, troubled, not knowing what she should do. Should his presence be reported to the police, or should she turn *herself* in—considering she'd spent a good part of the past twenty-four hours trespassing and spying?

When he reached the near bank, he hauled himself from the water, bringing with him a dazzling cascade of water. Not until he was pushing up to stand did Helen realize he was naked—a physical monument to his gender.

Unaccustomed to such bold masculinity, she let out a scandalized gasp, frightening birds from the branches above her. Losing her precarious balance on the balls of her feet, she toppled backward. Instinctively she rolled to her knees and jumped up, ready to run. But some wayward piece of her brain anchored her to the spot.

Instead of hightailing it home, her traitorous head turned to get one last glimpse of the mysterious stranger she'd intruded upon. With an insane mixture of relief and regret, she saw that he'd wrapped a towel at his waist. Even so, there was still a great deal of him to see. While her unruly gaze insisted on devouring him, she berated herself for such an unladylike breach of his privacy. Escaped convict or lunatic or whatever he might be, he didn't deserve to be ogled.

When their gazes clashed, his was flinty and guarded. "What the hell…" He ground out the words, recognition lifting one black eyebrow. "You again?" He began to move in her direction, his features accusing, resentful.

Dread swept through her, but she couldn't move. His stare was hypnotic, terrifyingly so. Her throat dry, she sucked in air, trying not to pass out. In an odd slow motion, he advanced on her, limping badly. Even as fear-numbed as her brain was, Helen caught on the fact that his left thigh was crisscrossed with crimson scars.

"What do you want?" He stumbled, and with a curse fell to one knee.

She took an impulsive step toward him, but her wits returned when he grabbed a wooden cane, hidden in the grass. As he righted himself, a vein in his temple throbbed. She sensed the effort was causing him great pain and her heart constricted with compassion.

"Looking for freaks, honey?" he said grittily. When she swung her glance to meet his again, she was stunned to see suffering shimmering there. "Get *pictures*, this time?"

He took another step toward her, and finally her self-protective instincts kicked in. She whirled away and ran for her life. Dashing home through the woods, she grew disgusted with herself. Why was she always running away like a panicked squirrel? The man was obviously unhappy and needed help. But he was so—so *hostile*.

She'd always been good with broken birds, sick kittens and even snapping dogs, but this mystery man was way out of her league. He had too much rage in him. She had a strong sense that not only his body was damaged, but his soul, too. It was a daunting sight to witness. Just the memory of his haunted stare scared her to death.

And there was always the chance he was an escaped murderer.

She swallowed, plunging her hands into her pockets. Besides, she had problems of her own. Some terrible time in the future—hopefully the far distant future—she would become Hirk Boggs's bride. Her lips quivery with despair, she mumbled, "Happy birthday to me."

By the time she arrived at the inn and was trudging up the back steps to the kitchen, her thoughts had drifted once again to the dark and damaged stranger. "What if he's not an escaped murderer? What if he's just a lonely, wounded man?'' she wondered aloud.

Unfortunately she had no answer. There was nothing she could do for him—coward that she was.

CHAPTER TWO

SUDDENLY it came to Helen. She knew who the angry stranger was. It had been niggling at the back of her mind all day; there was something so familiar about the man. And just as she began to blow out the twenty-one candles on her birthday cake, the truth hit her in a blinding flash.

She gasped aloud and stilled. Both of her sisters looked at her with concern. Elissa frowned. "Helen, baby, the object is to blow *out* the candles, not try to suck them in."

Lucy, who was standing beside Helen holding a cake knife, leaned down and touched her younger sister on the shoulder. "What's wrong, sweetie?"

Helen mumbled some fiction about a stitch in her side from painting all day.

"Well, you did work like you were driven." Lucy patted her. "I told you to take it easy, but you kept at it like the devil was prodding your backside."

Needing to stall, to get her mind straight on what she'd just realized, she blew out the candles. "I guess I—I learned my lesson," she finally mumbled.

Elissa reached across the small kitchen table, touching Helen's hand. "You've been great to work so hard without complaining, baby." She glanced at Lucy as the blonde removed candles and began to cut cake. "You both have. This place needed a lot of work when we bought it, and you two have been real troopers." Squeezing Helen's hand Elissa looked at her again, taking a moment to swallow. She seemed uncharacteristically lacking for words. "I owe you both more than I can repay—especially since each of you put up your share of the money Dad left us so I could have this inn." When Elissa glanced at Lucy, her green eyes were bright with tears. "Especially you, Luce. I mean, you're engaged. You could have used the money for a nest egg for you and Stadler."

Lucy smiled that gentle smile of hers, depositing chocolate cake on a dessert plate. "Don't be silly, Elissa. You know when you heard about this place being up for sale, we all decided it was a wonderful opportunity. Branson is growing by leaps and bounds; it would have been a crime to pass it up. Besides, you and Helen will do all the work while I'll be an absentee partner, once Stadler gets back to Kansas City." She handed a plate of cake to Elissa. "I'll be raking in my share without lifting a finger. It's fair."

Elissa blinked, taking the plate and returning her gaze to the birthday girl. "And you, baby. I moved you away from Kansas City, took the money you could have used for college."

"*Invested*, Elissa. Invested!" Helen grimaced at her sister's sudden show of doubt about her decision to move them all to Branson last summer. She shook her head at Elissa's misgivings. "When you realized law wasn't your dream, and running a country inn was, well, like Dad always said, you have to follow your dreams." Pushing up from the table, she retrieved the coffeepot and refilled their cups. "You already know my dream. I want to be a mama, and they don't teach that in college. Besides, I loved doing those baby-sitting jobs to help out while Dad was so sick. I didn't even mind changing dirty diapers, so I *know* being a mama is my true calling!''

She was smiling when thoughts of Hirk Boggs surfaced, and her pleasant expression was hard to maintain. *One day she would be the mama of Hirk Boggs's children.* With a hefty inhale, she returned the coffeepot to the counter and revived her smile. Deciding a subject change was in order, she kidded, ''Okay, people, this is *my* birthday party and I expect loot!''

Lucy rushed from the room to get the gifts, and Helen noticed that Elissa's face had brightened with her reassurances. Seeing that helped lift Helen's mood, too, though her new insight about the angry resident of the D'Amour mansion whirled around in her mind; it was so hard to believe she didn't dare voice it—not yet. Not until she was absolutely sure.

Lucy rushed in, her pretty face pink with excitement. She carried two packages. One was large, as though it contained clothing. The other was quite small. ''Okay, baby,'' Elissa said, as Lucy placed the gifts before their youngest sister. ''We don't have a lot of spending money, so remember, it's the thought that counts.''

Helen made a playful face. ''What? No diamond necklaces or expensive sports cars? How will I show my face in polite society?''

Her sisters laughed as Helen opened the little box from Elissa. She was moved almost to tears by what she saw. ''Why—why, Elissa.'' She looked up at her sister, blinking. ''It's a necklace.'' Helen had expected her practical big sister to have written up a Will for her or something. Nothing so—so poetic as this. She drew out a silver chain, lifting it up into better light. Twirling at the end of the chain was a dainty, silver replica of a human hand, cradling a puppy and kitten. "It's lovely," Helen whispered, truly touched.

"It's nothing much." Elissa shrugged. "I happened to see it in a curio shop in Branson, and thought of you and your thing about animals."

Helen's heart swelled as she fastened it around her neck. "It's perfect," she said with true affection. "I'd rather have this than a diamond necklace, any day."

Elissa smiled shyly, a rare expression for someone who had spent four years as a stubborn legal advocate for every type of low-life felon Kansas City could boast, before she'd decided that kind of dreary, thankless existence wasn't for her.

Helen opened the second package with dispatch to discover a white cardigan sweater. She squealed with glee. "So, this is what you've been hiding from me every time I came into your bedroom."

"Not bad for an amateur." Lucy tilted her head this way and that as she examined her handiwork. "You were my guinea pig. Now that I know I can do it, I'm going to start one for Stadler."

"Bigger, I hope," Helen teased as she stood and slipped into the cotton knit garment. Pretending the kitchen was a fashion runway, she did a few turns and poses to show off the sweater. "Am I not *perfection*?"

"Christy Brinkley, eat your heart out," Elissa quipped, and the Crosby girls burst out in a chorus of laughter.

Helen's birthday party was pleasant, and she even managed to go on acting as though nothing unusual was on her mind for the entire evening. It was a mammoth effort, and seemed like a year before Elissa and Lucy were finally in bed. Just before eleven o'clock, her compassionate nature battling down her fear, she sneaked back to the D'Amour mansion and left a basket of food on the kitchen steps. She was grateful when she made it all the way home without a single mishap.

Bolstered by her successful basket-drop last night after her birthday party, Helen decided that tonight she would repeat the act. This time she wasn't quite as fearful. After all, the dark stranger wasn't a devil or a murderer. Far from it.

Damien Lord was a hero.

Everyone in America knew of him, and was aware of the brave thing he'd done. So no matter how much his surly manner terrified her, she couldn't ignore the man. Not after she'd seen with her own eyes what his heroism had cost him.

Once her sisters were, again, safely asleep, she headed for the mansion. At the edge of the wood she stopped to catch her breath, staring at the huge edifice. Its silent majesty did nothing to calm her fear. Since no lights shined from any of the leaded glass windows, Helen decided Mr. Lord was probably asleep. She prayed he was. Tamping down a surge of panic, she stepped out of the sheltering trees.

Sprinting through the high grass, she angled toward the stone steps that led to a servants' porch half hidden in overgrown shrubs. She'd left last night's basket of food on the lowest step. Since it was gone, she decided her ploy had worked, and would work again.

When she reached the steps, her heart was hammering so badly she marveled that her rib cage didn't crumble to dust. Panting and anxious to get away, she set down her basket and turned to go, but crashed into something hard—something that hadn't been there a moment ago.

The "something" grasped her by the arm. "Don't

you want to collect your dishes?'' The question was asked with such venom, her captor might as well have been telling her he planned to strangle her. A scream clawed at her throat, but she couldn't make a sound. Waves of gray passed before her eyes making his strong, grim face waver and grow dim.

"Don't faint on me!" He tightened his hold. "If you do, you'll stay where you land. I can't carry you."

His warning revived her and she stiffened, struggled, but couldn't break his grip. "I'm not going to faint," she retorted, her voice stronger than it deserved to be.

A skeptical eyebrow quirked. "Yeah? And I'm the president of the United States."

She found herself being yanked up the steps. Because he had to use his cane, she wasn't dragged quickly, just insistently. "Where are you taking me?" She tried but failed again to release herself from his hold.

"We're getting last night's basket. And you're taking your latest care package back with you, too."

He pulled her through the servants' porch up two more steps into a room that must have been the staff's quarters. Only the dim moonlight leaching through dingy windows lit their way. The thud of his cane sounded hollow in her ears, the noise echoing off the bare walls. It seemed as though some sorrowful spirit had taken on substance and now walked with them in the darkness. "I'm not going any further!" she insisted, renewed alarm taking hold.

Ignoring her squirming protests, he dragged her through a short, dark hallway. Finally they emerged in what she recognized as a kitchen, yet even in the dimness she could tell that it was hardly up-to-date, and there was a layer of dust everywhere. The place hadn't been used for cooking in the recent past.

When Damien Lord abruptly let her go, she almost stumbled to her knees. "There!" He swept his hand toward a long table where last night's basket sat unopened. "Take it with you and don't come back."

Her glance caught on a light switch in a shaft of moonlight, and she automatically flicked it on. When she did, he jerked around to glare at her. For a split second she glimpsed bleakness in his gaze, but quickly his features closed, growing so malevolent, she shrank back.

"Shut that damn thing off!"

Every nerve in her body thrummed, warning her to escape, yet she didn't obey her instincts, didn't move. She knew if she were smart she'd run for her life. But nobody had ever accused her of being smart. "If—if it's because of your scars—"

His blaspheme cut her off every bit as effectively as the crashing swipe of his cane doused the light. "You think I'm *vain*?"

"I'm not talking about the scars that show," she blurted, then bit her lip. He was so angry the energy of his outrage radiated through the darkness searing her like a flame. She flinched, knowing she should go, knowing she was invading his privacy. But she couldn't help herself. Couldn't leave him alone, suffering. She wouldn't do that to an animal, so how could she do it to a human being?

"I don't need your pity!" Even in the gloom she could see his nostrils flare. "Pick up your mercy package and get out."

His vehemence flattened her against the wall, but she tried to hold on to her goal. She had come to help a good man in emotional pain, a vital man struck down in his prime, unable to do the work he loved any longer.

Damien Lord needed her, and she would *not* let him down.

Casting around in her mind for something to say, she tried to think of anything that would defuse his anger. Nothing inspired came to her so she offered meekly, "I—I didn't realize you owned this mansion."

He had turned away, having done with her. No doubt he'd expected her to run from his bitter rage as if she were a frightened mouse. When he shifted back, his expression showed incredulity. "If it's any of your business, it's a loan." His jaw bunched for a few seconds. "What do I have to do to get rid of you? *Shoot* you?"

Apprehension, quick and hot, cut off her breath, but she refused to heed the voice in her brain that was shouting that she flee like a madwoman. "I—I don't believe you'd shoot me," she whispered. "Because I know who you are, Mr. Lord, and I want to help."

He watched her for the slice of a moment, his expression stormy. "I don't need your help, either." This time when he turned from her, he began to limp away. "Get out."

There was no confusing his dismissal. It was absolute. She pulled her lips between her teeth as she watched him make slow progress across the cobwebbed kitchen. His hair was mussed and his clothes disheveled. As he walked into a shaft of moonlight streaming through a broken windowpane, the golden glow accented his torso. Through the wrinkled knit of his shirt she could detect power in his wide shoulders and see the coil of muscle in his arms as he supported much of his weight with the cane. Her gaze strayed down to his injured leg. He dragged it slightly, making a raspy sound on the gritty floor as he moved.

In her mind's eye she traveled back to the many times

she'd seen him on television. Damien Lord, one of CNN's top foreign correspondents, reporting hair-raising news stories amid the rubble of battle zones around the world—always so strong and self-assured, in iron control, showing no fear even in the face of flying bullets.

He'd been the heartthrob of millions of women with his dashing good looks and his nerve. But now, he was a wounded, angry recluse who hid from everyone and everything—even the light.

Yet, as weak and scarred as he was, Damien Lord was the most marvelous man she'd ever seen. Running a hand before her eyes, she pushed back that thought. A famous, sophisticated world traveler like him would never be interested in a meek, plain midwestern girl. He'd made it depressingly clear she was like a gnat in need of swatting.

Besides, destiny had spoken. Hirk Boggs was her true love. A wave of depression engulfed her, but she forced herself to shake it off, her nurturing side coming to the fore. If Damien Lord thought he could get rid of her with a few snarls, then he had another "think" coming.

He'd reached the far door when she found her voice. "You need to eat to build yourself up."

He stilled, half turned, then seemed to think better of it. "Are you still here?"

She felt a protective stirring inside her. Intent on going to him, she pushed away from the wall, but discovered her legs were shaky. She had to stop and hold on for a second, taking in a huge draught of air. "You remind me of Cracker—my three-legged dog."

She could only see his profile, but even from that angle, his expression was so forbidding it took all her courage to push away from the wall and walk toward him.

"Three-legged dog?" he repeated with dark irony. "How accurate—but insensitive."

It took her a second to grasp his meaning—his cane was like a third leg. Disturbed that he'd taken her comment so wrong, she cried, "That's not what I meant! When—when I found Cracker he *acted* as badly as you're acting."

Damien shifted around, using his cane to support himself. He was the image of a wounded grizzly. "Do you have a death wish, kid?"

Her heart was beating erratically and she felt faint, but she continued her determined approach even in the face of his animosity. At this moment he even resembled Cracker a little. His posture and demeanor were savage and threatening.

He hadn't shaved today. His chin was dark with stubble, enhancing his dangerous image. She found it hard to speak in the face of such an awesome, masculine presence, but at last she managed to shake her head. "When I found Cracker—" her voice splintered but she hurried on "—he growled and snapped, too. But that was because he was frightened and hurt—and hungry."

Damien's scowl deepened, but when he didn't respond she forged on. "I'm a good cook, Mr. Lord, and I plan to come here every evening with a meal for you."

"Like hell you are!"

She lifted her chin with bravado. "And—and I'm leaving the basket I brought tonight. If you don't eat every scrap—you'll regret it."

He turned in her direction, the gesture openly hostile. "And just *how* will I regret it?"

She had no idea. It was a shame he didn't fall for idle threats. Uneasy, she tried to figure out what this man's Achilles' heel might be. Then it came to her—the thing he most feared. Though she wasn't proud of herself, she met his glower with one of her own, promising with soft menace, "I'll tell."

His chin came up as though he'd been punched, and she knew she'd found his weakness. The last thing he wanted was to be found. He would be deluged by curiosity seekers, and he hated the thought of that. Raking a hand through his hair, he glanced away, then turned to scowl at her again. "Blackmail is an ugly business, kid."

She drew a breath, the first she'd taken in a long time, it seemed, for she was dizzy. But she was also elated. *She had him where she wanted him.* "Then you'll eat?"

Though his stare was angry, there was a subtle change in his demeanor, like a cornered wolf discovering he had no escape. "You'd better keep your mouth shut."

She nodded. "This is for your own good, you know."

He snorted contemptuously. "If I hear that one more damned time—" He cut himself off and indicated the exit with a jerk of his head. "Get the hell out."

"I'll be back tomorrow."

"I'm thrilled."

"You don't have to be happy about it, you just have to eat."

The curse he muttered was crude, but it hardly fazed her. He was simply snarling again, like Cracker had done. The important thing was that Damien had promised he would *eat*, and that knowledge buoyed her spirits.

She ran home with a smile on her face and a new feeling of purpose in her heart. Fate couldn't be so cruel to reward Damien Lord for his heroism by ruining his life. She would never believe that. He was a brave, caring man who deserved the best. Even though he'd lost an eye, and would always carry his physical scars, she vowed to help him heal emotionally—to find himself, again—so that one day, he could reach out and accept the happiness due him.

After a week, her secret was becoming hard to keep. Elissa and Lucy were starting to think she had a tapeworm, or worse, since she spent so much time in the kitchen cooking up food that quickly disappeared. So, this morning, while Elissa and Lucy ran errands in Branson, Helen decided she'd better take Mr. Lord breakfast, today, instead of dinner, and get it over before her sisters got back.

There had been an early-morning rain shower, so she opted to walk along the asphalt road and steer clear of muddy spots in the woods. It was her bad luck, as she entered the weathered circular driveway of the D'Amour mansion, that Hirk Boggs came rattling up behind her in his butter and egg van.

He braked before the mansion's main entrance and hopped out, putting a finger to the brim of his straw hat. Nodding, he grinned at her. "Morning, Miss Helen." His lisp seemed more pronounced than ever and the saliva he sprayed with each *s* seemed to fly further from his lips. She kept a safe distance. "What ya doing here with a picnic basket?" he asked. "Welcoming our mysterious new neighbor?"

Though she felt a rush of nausea at the knowledge that Hirk was her romantic future, she tried to smile. It was apparent from his remark that he'd never seen the mansion's occupant. And since his assumption about her being there with a welcoming basket was as good as any, she nodded. "Yes—I thought bringing a few things over would be the neighborly thing to do."

Hirk ambled around to the back of his van and opened the door, pulling out two dozen eggs. "You're a mighty fine young lady to think of it, Miss Helen." He gave her a look that she feared held a trace of affection, and she shivered. Luckily Hirk didn't see her reaction, for he was loping up the stone steps to deposit the eggs on the deep porch that protected the arched entry.

When he shambled back down, he paused before her. His gaunt cheeks were pink, and Helen's woman's intuition warned her it was not from the exertion of depositing the eggs on the top step. She stiffened as she watched his Adam's apple bob up and down. *Oh, no! He's going to ask me to go out with him!*

"Miss Helen?" He stopped and shifted from one foot to another. She pulled her lips between her teeth and waited. There was no fighting Destiny. When he still hadn't spoken for a full minute, she couldn't stand it any longer and prodded, "Yes, Hirk?"

He managed another uncertain grin. "Uh, well I was wonderin' if you was going to the Chamber of Commerce dance the first Saturday night in October?"

She transferred the heavy basket to her other hand, sweeping her lashes down to hide her dejection. Once the stalling movement was completed, she looked him straight in the eyes and made herself smile. It wasn't her best smile, but under the circumstances, quite good. "Why—no, Hirk. I haven't been asked."

He toyed with his frayed collar for a few ponderous seconds, his cheeks growing ruddier. "Uh, no kidding? Well, I was thinkin' maybe—you might like to go with me, then?"

Sucking in a breath, she nodded, sure that using her voice would betray her lack of enthusiasm. After another few heartbeats, she managed to say, "I'd love to, Hirk."

If she hadn't known better, she might have believed it was true.

His grin broadened to display more of his gums than Helen cared to see. Unable to help herself, she dropped her gaze.

"Well, Miss Helen, that's just *fine*."

She nodded again, switching her basket from hand to hand as he added, "I'll pick you up at seven."

She compelled herself to look at him. "Seven. Great."

He said something more, but her mind had gone numb, unwilling or unable to deal with the finality of it all. Apparently Fate didn't plan to waste much time pushing them together.

She realized he was waving goodbye as he chugged off, and she returned his farewell. When he was out of sight she squeezed her eyes shut, sternly telling herself that there was probably much, *much* more to Hirk than met the eye. This dance would allow her to begin discovering all of his hidden, charming qualities.

Pulling herself together, she opened her eyes, then stilled when she detected movement on the porch. Apprehension slithered along her spine.

"Young love?" came a deep, scoffing voice.

She jerked around to confirm her fear. Damien Lord was barely visible in the deep shade of a stone pillar. "Have you been there all along?" Her face stung with humiliation. Why she was embarrassed was a mystery to her. What difference did it make that this man had seen her accept a date.

He stepped into the sunlight, and Helen caught her breath. He wasn't wearing a shirt, and his jeans were low-slung, revealing more taut belly than she was accustomed to running into.

"Pardon me for being on my own porch," he said dryly.

The way he looked her up and down made her have to fight an urge to cover herself, though she had on more clothes than he did. Maybe her loose cotton T-shirt and cutoff jeans looked untidy, all streaked with paint, but they were clean. Besides, she hadn't wanted to arouse her sister's suspicions by putting on a dress.

His narrowed glance fell to her wicker hamper. "I thought I was rid of you until tonight."

She hoisted the basket more securely in both fists and trudged up the steps. "If I'm to keep your secret, I can't always stick to a schedule." She picked up the eggs and placed them into the hamper before indicating the door. "Shall we go?"

"We?" His tone was as ominous as his frown.

Though his never-ending belligerence unsettled her, she lifted her chin defiantly. "I'm cooking this time. Breakfast is the most important meal of the day, you know."

"Little girls who can't mind their own business can get hurt, you know."

She smirked at him. "I see you're in a better mood, today." Turning the ornate knob, she opened the door. Before stepping inside, she looked over her shoulder. "It's because you're *eating* better."

Though his eyebrows knit a fraction further, he didn't deny it.

"So, how do you like your eggs?"

"Alone."

She laughed. *Actually laughed.* Stepping inside, she left the door ajar so that he could follow. "It's good to see you're getting a sense of humor back," she teased, heading toward the kitchen. Though she didn't catch what he muttered, she had a feeling that was for the best.

Lighthearted, she wiped away the worst of the dust and began preparing Damien's breakfast. He didn't grace her with his glowering company as she went about her work, and she wasn't surprised. But neither was she worried. He would be there when she set the hot food on the table. She knew that as surely as she knew he wouldn't really do her harm.

She'd learned an important lesson this past week—about herself. Helen Rose Crosby was a grown-up, adult person who *could* be brave when the reason was important enough. Oh, she wasn't kidding herself. She was no hero, like Damien, but she wasn't a complete coward, either. That had been a nice thing to discover. She'd also learned one other important thing. It seemed that snarling, injured men were not so different from snarling, injured dogs, after all.

Helen sat across the freshly polished oak table, smiling at Damien as he silently ate. He'd put on a shirt before joining her in the kitchen—the first sign that civility still lurked inside this brooding beast. That small act had reaffirmed her faith that time and care would uncloak the self-assured, productive man, again. Her heart turned over with gladness at the thought. When he peered at her and refreshed his scowl, she only smiled.

As he finished off the last of his breakfast, she jumped up. "More orange juice?"

He scanned her, his expression as dark as a storm cloud. "I've had so much now that I couldn't get scurvy if I never saw citrus fruit again."

She ignored his grumbling and got the container from

the refrigerator, refilling his glass. "You need lots of vitamin C."

"Look, kid, I know all about vitamin C. I *interviewed* Linus Pauling."

"Who?"

He shook his head. "Just how old are you, kid?"

"Stop calling me *kid*! I'm twenty-one!" She plunked the empty carton on the table and shoved the glass at him. "Drink!"

With a groan, he struggled to stand. "Forget it, you little Nazi, I'm swimming in the stuff, now."

Relenting, she leaned against the table and crossed her arms before her. "Okay. I admit you ate a good breakfast."

He adjusted his cane to better support his weight. "Now will you go?"

"I have to clean up."

She could tell he was gritting his teeth by the bunching muscles in his jaw. "I'll do it."

She rolled her eyes. "Sure. The place was spotless when I came in here."

His shrug was weary. "Okay, do what you have to do."

When he turned his back, her heart sank. She didn't suppose she should expect his thanks. After all, she was blackmailing him, forcing herself and her food on him. Dejected, she picked up the orange juice glass and began to pour it back into the carton.

"Is that Boggs guy your boyfriend?"

She was so startled that he was speaking to her she sloshed juice on the table. Oddly short of breath, she set the carton and the glass down and looked at him. He was leaning on the hardwood counter, eyeing her speculatively.

"Why would you ask that?"

He half grinned, but the look was more irascible than amused. "It would explain something."

She frowned in confusion. "What would it explain?"

He shrugged, the rise and fall of his wide shoulders drawing her gaze. "Nothing. Never mind."

Irritation heated her cheeks but she squelched it. At least he was making conversation, however minimal. She had a thought and decided to voice it. "Why don't you go to the dance, too? My sisters, Elissa and Lucy, would love to drive you."

The suffering that flashed in his gaze reminded her of his aversion to meeting people. "I'm not in the mood to be stared at."

She decided it was best to get the subject out in the open. "You wouldn't be."

Hostility fairly radiated from him, the firm set of his jaw made it clear that he had no intention of discussing the matter. Blinking, she stumbled a defensive step backward before she got hold of herself. *She would not chicken out now*! "You really wouldn't be stared at— not after the first few minutes," she insisted. "After all, *I* don't stare at you."

"You?" His chuckle was a blend of bitterness and incredulity. "You're a fine example of the mainstream. If our toothless friend, Mr. Boggs, is one of your boyfriends, I'm afraid your taste runs to oddities."

She was so astonished that he assumed she had *several* boyfriends, she could only gape at him.

He pursed his lips. "On the other hand, you have a pretty good stare when you work at it."

She swallowed, embarrassed. "I—I wasn't…"

"Forget it." He shoved away from the counter. "I'm not going to any dances." Tapping his cane against the floor, he drew it to her attention. "My tango's a little rusty."

She flushed. "Oh—right..."

When her glance returned to his face, she was surprised to see him watching her. There was no real scowl marring his features, yet his expression couldn't be described as pleasant, either. He was just looking at her. "So, why are you going to a dance with a man who's forty if he's a day, who looks like a cartoon character and has the intelligence of gravel?"

She cringed at his bluntness. "That's none of your business."

"None of my business?" His grin was slow and ripe with shrewd skepticism. "I'm surprised a little blackmailer would admit some things aren't anybody's business."

He could use his words like a knife, and the insight stabbed. She spun away, and with clumsy fingers gathered up his plate and silverware. Avoiding his probing gaze, she marched to the sink. Unfortunately, when she got there, she realized the move had brought her closer to him.

"So what is it about our toothless friend that you find seductive?"

So upset she couldn't talk, she yanked on the spigot. The handle squeaked in protest and the pipes rattled and honked for a few seconds before water spurted out.

"Is he good in bed?"

She gasped, whirling toward him. His grin was teasing, and a long slashing dimple appeared in his undamaged cheek. The image was unexpectedly stimulating, and something went haywire with gravity because she found herself clutching the counter to keep from crashing to the floor.

An eyebrow rose. "What? None of my business, again?"

When her equilibrium returned, she shifted away and began to scrub the plate. Silence billowed around her, smothering her until she could hardly breathe. She could feel his stare. His *amused* stare! "Hirk is a very *nice* person," she finally spat. After all, Damien was taunting her about her future husband!

"I've always heard nice guys finish last."

She stopped scrubbing and faced him, squaring her shoulders. "They shouldn't," she retorted, honestly. "That's why I'm *here*."

Any teasing in his attitude vanished like an extinguished match. There was no question that he'd heard her meaning loud and clear, but neither was there any question that he didn't plan to go down that road.

The room became oppressively close, tension crackling in the air between them. He stared her down, trying to intimidate her, to make her back off, his condemnation tainting the very air. Her chest hurt with the effort it took to catch her breath, and her courage drained away.

No! She couldn't allow that. Even though she was picturing herself being thrown bodily out a window, she blurted, "Look, Mr. Lord, you did a fine thing. You're a hero. It's not *fair* that you should suffer like this."

"You believe life should be fair?" Shuttered aloofness rode his gaze again, as though he were trying to distance himself emotionally. "Then, maybe I should ask for my money back."

Beneath the barbed sarcasm she detected his anguish, and it had a profound effect on her. She reached out to touch his arm, but he threw off her hand with a curse, his vehemence frightening her.

"*Dammit*!" He towered there, his gaze flashing menacing denial. "Don't look at me like that! I did what I did instinctively. There was nothing heroic about it."

The depth of his passion made her feel helpless and self-doubt shrouded her, washing away her feelings of accomplishment. Who did she think she was, opening such deep wounds? Was she being selfish, wanting to prove she was grown up by insinuating herself into his life? Maybe injured men weren't that much like injured animals after all. Human beings were much more complicated creatures. She wrung her hands in confusion and worry.

Even as stormy seconds passed, even as the electricity between them grew to deadly levels, she remained rooted near him. She couldn't let go of her desire to befriend him, though it was clear she was meddling where she wasn't wanted. Could she be doing him harm—delaying his healing with her interference?

Her thoughts tumbled back to the heroic thing he'd done. She recalled the scene—that day last May—when Damien Lord risked his life to save a child from a hail of mortar fire. The whole tragic incident had been captured on live television during a CNN report.

She attempted a dry swallow, wanting to voice her feelings. "Look, Mr. Lord—" The sound she made was husky and weak. "No matter how loudly you deny it, your courage was witnessed by millions. There's no doubt that you saved a young life by putting your own in danger."

His jaw was as tense as her nerves, but when he started to speak, she cut in, fairly shouting, "So many people saw that little boy wander into harm's way—right there on camera—while you were doing your report. There were at least twenty people there who could have done something, but it was you—you alone—who risked everything, saving the boy, protecting him with your body." She stopped herself before adding, "*And in the process, you were terribly wounded.*" He didn't need to be reminded about that.

The recollection bolstered her resolve. She wasn't wrong in what she was doing. Kindness could never be wrong. That knowledge gave her a crazy sort of strength. "Don't you see? That's how heroes are made—they jump in to help without thinking."

He grunted contemptuously. "Yeah, and look at the perks." He swept a hand from his eyepatch to his cane. "A half-blind cripple who can make children scream just by walking into a room." He flicked his tortured gaze away. "Go home, little girl. You can't give me what I need."

His insult slammed into her heart, doing damage. She knew he was lashing out, hiding his pain by inflicting it on her. But, even knowing that, it was hard to take. She willed herself to appear composed, though inside she was a churning mess. "I think I can," she murmured.

"And you probably believe in the tooth fairy, too."

Even though she was near tears, and instinctively knew that situations of high emotion weren't good times to make decisions, she came to a decision, anyway—one she'd been struggling with for days. "I'm not coming back here."

His stare narrowed at the rancor in her tone, and he leaned toward her. His features grew speculative, his lips curving in a dubious smile. "And to what do I owe this happy news?"

His face was mere inches from hers. The urge was strong in her to retreat, to step out of the minefield of his bitterness and frustration, but she held her ground.

He was pleased with the prospect of never seeing her again, and that stung as badly as any insult he had thrown at her so far. She had no idea she could be this upset by such undisguised pleasure at the idea of getting rid of her. So, it was with the tiniest bit of satisfaction that she informed him, "You're coming to the inn for dinner tomorrow night. I can't keep up this charade. My sisters think I have an eating disorder."

He straightened abruptly. "You're not serious."

The shock in his voice almost made her smile. "I'm completely serious, Mr. Lord. But don't worry. My sisters will be discreet."

"No way, kid." His glare was murderous. "Not in a million years."

"If you don't come, I'll *tell*." She bit her lip. That sounded awfully childish, but she couldn't worry about that, now. Damien's aversion to being discovered was her only leverage, and she had to use it—for his own good. Otherwise she sensed he wouldn't eat. He'd just wander around in the drafty old mansion like a brooding ghost. "We'll expect you at seven, sharp."

She was rewarded with a profanity.

CHAPTER THREE

HELEN checked her watch. It was ten minutes *after* seven. She rubbed her neck. Her shoulders and back burned with tension; her head throbbed. She'd been tense all day with nervous anticipation, and now Damien wasn't even coming.

She'd volunteered to make dinner, which suited Elissa and Lucy just fine. They both admitted Helen was the best cook of the three of them. She'd insisted her sisters take relaxing baths and change into dresses for dinner. She'd told them she had a surprise, but revealed nothing more.

She had also taken great care with her appearance, and thought she looked quite sophisticated in her beige cotton turtleneck and plaid wrap skirt. She felt a twinge of doubt, scraping the toe of one loafer against the door. Why on earth did she choose the word sophisticated? She wasn't trying to impress Damien Lord—just *feed* him.

Checking her watch again, she stared through the etched glass in the front door, straining to see through the gathering darkness for any sight of him along the road.

"Dinner smells good," Elissa said, startling her with her silent approach across the painter's drop cloth. "I'm starving. Couldn't we eat?"

Helen spun around, calming her heart rate before she tried her voice. "Uh—just five more minutes?"

Elissa's expression grew curious. "Are you expecting someone?"

"Well…" Helen felt her cheeks flush. "I did invite somebody…"

Elissa tossed her head, her Titian hair catching the light. With that crown of fire, even in her neutral tweed suit, she lit up a room. "Oh, Helen, baby, is this another of your charity causes?" Elissa plunked her fists on her slender hips. "Remember the last time? The guy stole mother's silver trivet. His way of saying thanks, I guess."

Helen gulped. "Well, er, I don't think…"

"I'm afraid that's true, baby. You don't think." Elissa placed a sisterly arm around her shoulders. "You can't fix everything and everybody with trust and kindness. Believe me, I've worked with some of the world's worst dregs. You don't always get repaid with—"

Cracker's sharp bark made them jump. With new hope flooding her heart, Helen dashed away from her sister. Cracker was at the back door, barking at something outside. Of course, Damien would come through the woods. She should have known he would go to any lengths to keep from being seen—even drag his injured leg along a craggy, woodland path. Her guilt at that realization was short-lived; she was so overcome with relief that he was actually here.

"It's him!" she cried, unable to hide her delight.

"Who?" Elissa was following so closely Helen was afraid she planned to block the door and refuse to allow this newest charity case inside to eat their food and steal their family heirlooms, even though most were still in packing boxes.

Helen reached the back door and looked out, at first seeing nothing unusual. But as she squinted into the twilight duskiness of the wood beyond the picket fence, there he was. Almost imperceptible in the gloaming, the tall stranger stood silently, one hand resting on the gate.

She smiled, satisfaction rushing through her. Elissa pulled aside the lace window covering so that she could get a clear view. "Oh my…" Her whisper was tinged with trepidation. "He looks awfully big. Are you sure this is wise?"

Helen squeezed her sister's arm reassuringly. "Just wait and see." She flung the door wide and rushed out to snag her reluctant visitor before he could think better of being there. "Get Lucy," she called. "We can eat, now."

The smell of wallpaper paste clung to the air in the formal dining room, mixing with the hearty scents of roast beef, new potatoes and carrots. Helen had placed Damien at the head of the table, with herself on his right and her sisters on his left. The meal was half over, cloaked in strained silence, the demeanor of the gathering dictated by their solemn guest.

Helen was accustomed to his hostile manner and was all smiles as she offered more coffee. Lucy and Elissa sat like stone statues, hardly touching their food. They were dumbfounded by the fact that the famous hero, Damien Lord, was sitting at their table, glowering like a wary, wounded wolf.

Helen couldn't blame her sisters for their speechlessness. It was like having the president of the United States drop by for tea. Well, maybe it was more like having the president drop by for tea—at gunpoint. "Would you care for more potatoes, Mr. Lord?" Her buoyancy over his compliance still sang through her veins. Even his lethal glares didn't faze her.

He looked as if he hadn't slept, hadn't shaved and had kept his clothes wadded in knots as some kind of New Age, texture statement. Even so, he was there, and he was eating. She was as happy as a schoolgirl with the highest grade in class. She'd worked hard for this, and Damien Lord's hearty appetite was her reward.

With her query, he shifted his glance her way, his expression filled with umbrage. "No," he finally answered, and with that one word, turned back to his plate. Helen noticed Elissa and Lucy exchange troubled glances, and she grinned their way. "How about you, two? More potatoes?"

They shook their heads in unison, then Lucy, uncomfortable with discord of any kind, cleared her throat. Helen knew she was going to try, again, to make their guest feel comfortable. She doubted Lucy's efforts would succeed, yet she held her breath, hoping. Lucy's natural sweetness was hard for anyone to resist.

The blonde smiled at Damien. "I understand you're from New York, Mr. Lord." She paused for him to respond. When he merely slanted her a narrowed gaze that said he didn't give a damn what she understood, she swallowed several times, but went on bravely. "Our— our mother was from New York. She died of leukemia when Helen was four, but all these years that charming New York accent has reminded me of mother."

Damien lifted a skeptical brow, as though dubious that anyone would think the New York accent was particularly charming, then lowered his gaze to his plate, eating the last chunk of potato.

"But, of course, Mr. Lord doesn't have that accent any longer," Elissa added. "Trained TV journalists have to cultivate any regional dialect out of their voices. Isn't that right, Mr. Lord?" She smiled helpfully, as though her vigilant cheerfulness would force words from his mouth.

The question hung in the air, unanswered, as he sat there surly and sullen, his gaze on his plate.

Helen was far from surprised by his rudeness and passed her sisters a thanks-for-trying look. Patting her lips with her napkin, she laid it aside. "Well, since we're finished…" Overhauling her smile, she stood. "I have a freshly baked apple pie for dessert. À la mode, anybody?"

She was met with wide-eyed muteness by her sisters. Damien's angry stare remained on his plate. She grinned. "À la mode all around, then." As she turned to go, she heard shuffling. "I'll help!" both Elissa and Lucy called at the same time, halfway out of their chairs, but she waved them off. "You two stay and chat with Mr. Lord."

She almost laughed at their helpless expressions as they sat down. It was as though they were pleading, "*How can we chat with him? He won't even look at us!*"

The three sisters and their guest ate dessert in stark silence. Once Damien's pie was gone, he gave Helen a sidelong glance, then pushed himself up from the table. She jumped up, too, and he snarled, "I've done what you asked. I'm leaving."

She nodded. "Of course, Mr. Lord. It was a pleasure to have you." She turned to her sisters. "Wasn't it."

They looked pained, but nodded. "Pleasure," murmured Lucy.

"Certainly—was…" echoed Elissa.

Both women stood, smiling weakly. "Do come again," Elissa offered, belatedly holding out a hand.

His smoldering glare was his only answer, gripping

both Elissa and Lucy in its snare. "Don't tell *anyone* I was here."

Helen's sisters shifted to give her a puzzled glance. When she nodded at them, they looked back at Damien, Elissa voicing their agreement. "If that's what you—"

"Goodbye." His snarl cut off further discussion. Shifting, he leveled his glower on Helen. "Now, will you leave me alone?"

She'd hoped his attitude would have mellowed by this time, and gave him a pleading look. He met it with ice. "Oh, Mr. Lord, can't you get it through your head that all we want to do is help?"

His jaw shifted from side to side and his nostrils flared. "And can't you get it through yours that I don't want your help?" He presented her with his back, trudging out of the dining room toward the rear door. Luckily for Helen, his injured leg didn't allow him a swift escape.

Sensing she'd pushed this man about as far as he planned to be pushed, she didn't dare order him to come back every day. Gathering her courage, she ventured, "Next Friday? Same time?"

He didn't turn, didn't respond.

She gritted her teeth. She hated threatening him, but he gave her no choice, the stubborn brute. "Remember, if you don't come—"

"I know—you'll tell."

She experienced a skitter of hope. "Then you'll come?"

"Do I have a choice?"

"No."

He didn't see her satisfied expression, for it was at that instant that he slammed the door at his back, and was gone.

When she turned around, her smile faded, for her two sisters were advancing on her, deep concern on their faces. Her first instinct was to run into the kitchen or down the stairs to her room, but she knew she'd have to face them sooner or later. She leaned against the door, suddenly very tired. She attempted a smile, but had a feeling her expression was more of a wince than a grin. "Well, how did you like him?"

Lucy's exhale was almost a moan, but it was Elissa, who took up the conversational reins. "Helen, baby, you've brought home a lot of strays over the years, but this one is—is..." She took Helen's hands and squeezed. "Baby, this guy is really something. I've never seen anybody so mad at the world." She shook her head, at a loss—an unnatural state for Elissa. A few hushed seconds passed before she cautioned, "I know how soft-hearted you are, baby, and—and—well, Damien Lord is so..." She shrugged, her expression troubled. "He's so—male! Just don't let your compassion for him get all mixed up with—" She eyed heaven, shaking her head. "What I'm *trying* to say is, don't get a little-girl crush on this man. He's from a different world and one day he'll heal and leave here."

Helen was stunned by the advice. Why, the idea that she would make the mistake of falling in love with Damien was crazy. She grinned to reassure her sisters, but the expression faltered. "I'm not that naïve. I know he'll get better and go away. But right now he needs a friend, and I want to be that friend."

Always the peacemaker, Lucy touched Helen's face sympathetically. "This is an awfully nice thing you're trying to do. It's clear the man needs—needs to know people care." She patted Helen's cheek. "If anybody can get him to smile again, you and your pot roast can."

Elissa squeezed Helen's hands. "As long as you understand the way things are." Letting go of her fingers, she took a step back. "Okay, end of lecture. I guess it's time Lucy and I got to cleaning up those dishes."

Helen had a thought as her sisters headed into the kitchen. "Elissa, who's Linus Pauling?"

The redhead looked back. "What?"

"Linus Pauling. Did he discover vitamin C or something?"

Elissa's expression grew confused. "What in the world brought that up?"

Helen clutched her hands together. "When I was trying to get Mr. Lord to drink his orange juice he said he interviewed Linus Pauling so he knew all about vitamin C."

Elissa laughed. "Oh, I get it. Well, let's see. If I remember right, Linus Pauling won a couple of Nobel prizes. One was for chemistry. I don't remember what the other one was for. Anyway, he advocated large doses of vitamin C for good health."

Helen pursed her lips, feeling stupid. "Oh…"

Elissa eyed her sister curiously. "What's the matter now?"

"He thinks I'm a kid."

"I assume you mean Mr. Lord, not Mr. Pauling." Elissa's features became thoughtful and she shifted to face Helen. Placing a hand at her little sister's chin, Elissa forced her to look into her own shrewd, green eyes. "I thought you said you were too smart to get a crush on that guy."

Helen's cheeks heated, and she sidestepped away from Elissa's touch. "Don't be silly! You treat me like a kid, too, but I don't have a crush on *you*."

"Mmm-hmm." Elissa didn't sound convinced.

"Believe what you want!" Helen's mood plummeted as she slid by her sisters, descending the steps on the run to her room. "I only want to be Mr. Lord's *friend*."

That was absolutely, positively true. And someday soon she would tell Elissa and Lucy about Hirk Boggs, her true love. That would prove she wasn't getting a crush on Mr. Lord.

As she slammed into her room, she experienced a tinge of regret at the recollection of Hirk and her pre-ordained future with him. Irritated at herself for balking at her destiny, she declared aloud, "Someday—very soon—I'll tell them about Hirk!"

Seven-thirty—and Damien had not appeared at the back gate. Helen was fuming. Her marinated trout fillets had turned into trout jerky and weren't fit to eat. How could he be so insensitive?

She marched into the dining room where Lucy and Elissa were waiting. "I can't stand his stubborn, wounded-bear act. We're going to get him."

Even Elissa, the tough as nails lawyer, gave her sister an appalled look. "You can't mean that, baby. We can't go drag the man here. It would be kidnapping."

Lucy smiled wanly. "Not to mention the fact that he's pretty big. We'd have to knock him out. I think that's probably against some laws, too."

Helen balled her fists at her sides. "What are you saying? That we just forget him? Let him stay there and starve?"

Elissa stood, her expression stern but compassionate. "He's not starving. Joe at the Handy Mart said he'd had instructions to send a bag of groceries out to the mansion every few days. The man's fine. He just wants to be left alone."

Helen was hurt that her sisters were against her in this. "Then—then you won't help me? You won't go with me?"

Lucy's pretty face colored with alarm. "You don't mean you're actually going?"

Helen hadn't realized she had such a stubborn streak in her, but she nodded. "I'm driving over right now."

Lucy gave Elissa a worried look. "What can we do?"

The redhead shifted her glance out the front window, frowning. It was her lawyer's argumentative expression and *never* meant surrender.

As far as Helen was concerned, the time for argument was past. She didn't plan to hang around to debate the issue. Her mind made up, she spun around, sailing out of the dining room. "Don't bother trying to stop me!" Snatching the car keys from the newly built reception desk in the entry hall, she grabbed the front doorknob. "I'll bring him back here if I have to sneak up on his blind side and hit him with a chair."

"He'll sue you," Elissa warned.

"Okay, fine."

"Oh, dear, Elissa," Lucy fretted. "We can't let her do this."

Helen was halfway out the door when Elissa called, "We're coming with you!"

Helen felt a surge of relief that her sisters weren't deserting her, but she wasn't a fool. They might be coming, but only to try to dissuade her. She didn't slow her pace as she rushed to their aging sedan. If they wanted to come along, they would have to run to catch up.

"Oh—my *Lord*!"

Helen heard Elissa's shrill cry in the distance. Though she'd just entered the library at the far end of the mansion, she twirled around, her heart in her throat, as she dashed toward the sound of her sister's voice.

The servants' porch had been unlocked so they had entered there, calling Damien's name. When he didn't answer, Helen had begun to fear that he'd suddenly decided to leave.

The women had split up to make a search, Elissa taking the upstairs and Lucy the other half of the huge downstairs. Now Elissa was calling Helen's name. Her pulse hammering in her brain, she darted up the staircase in the entryway, then came to a staggering halt when she reached the second-floor landing. Elissa was hunched over Damien, who lay there on his back. So still. Blood oozed from a gash at his temple. A broken section of stair railing lay on his chest.

"We'd better not move him." Elissa pressed her fingers lightly against his carotid artery. "His pulse is strong, thank heaven." She looked up at Helen. "Call Doc Holly."

She flew down the stairs nearly smashing into Lucy. After she made the call, it seemed like an eternity before the retired doctor, who lived nearby, had examined Damien and given them the good news that he not only would live, but could be moved. Swearing the doctor to secrecy, the sisters managed to get a groggy Damien to the inn and into bed.

Damien was fully conscious by the time Doc Holly finished dressing his wound. The physician frowned down at the younger man, shaking his head. "That was quite a tumble, young fella'. You're lucky you're not dead."

Damien grimaced, peering up at him. "You sure, Doc?"

His frown deepening, the doctor turned to Helen, hovering nearby, and ushered her out of the room to give her instructions.

After he was gone, she gathered her nerve and reentered the freshly painted, front bedroom they'd assigned to Damien. He looked big and out-of-place in the lacy Victorian chamber, lying beneath her great-grand-mother's Wedding Ring quilt. By his scowling profile, she had a feeling he felt out-of-place, too. Putting on her happiest face she asked, "Hungry?"

He turned at the sound of her voice, then grimaced at the pain the move caused. When he didn't answer, she pulled a high-back chair next to the bed and sat down. "How about some trout jerky?"

He squinted at her. "All out of chicken soup?"

Was that an attempt at humor? She laughed. "I can fix some, if that's what you want."

He turned away with a wince, to stare out the window at the darkness. "What is it with you, kid? Trying to earn a Girl Scout badge or something?"

She counted to ten to quell her flash of anger. He was a hard man to reach! *Darn him.* But she wouldn't let his snarling get her down, because that was all it was—just snarling to hide pain. She sat forward, but didn't dare touch his arm, though the urge was strong. "Stop me if you've heard this before, Mr. Lord, but I'm trying to help."

His jaw tightened and there was silence for a long, drawn out moment before he said something. She frowned, not sure she'd heard him right.

"What?" she asked, her voice tight with amazement.

When he shifted her way again, he was frowning, but there was a hint of civility in his gaze. "I said, thanks." Though his tone was irascible, she knew he meant it.

His situation was hard for him to face—that he was

so weak and sick he needed help even to sit up. It would be almost impossible for any man to deal with such infirmity, especially a man who'd been so vital, who had known such international prominence. Helen had a feeling this was the first time in his life he wasn't in control of his world. And now, flat on his back in a prissy room, with no say in the matter, he had to feel as frustrated and useless as a man could feel. Still, he'd said thank you.

Suddenly she was so full of emotion she couldn't trust her voice. Managing a nod, hot tears stung her eyes, and she blinked them back.

He chuckled, then groaned at the discomfort it caused. "You don't take expressions of gratitude well, do you, kid." He fingered the gauze dressing at his right temple. "I'd growl at you, but it hurts too much."

She smiled tremulously, and stood. "You know what they say." Swiping at a tear, she put on a lighthearted front. "No pain, no gain." She turned to go. "I'll fix you that soup, but it'll be canned."

"Damn," he said, but didn't sound as if he really cared.

Her composure returning, she stopped at the door, looking back. "Haven't you heard, Mr. Lord? Life *isn't* fair." She flashed him a teasing grin. "Want your money back?"

He eyed her narrowly. "Smart-mouth, kid."

Saturday morning, Helen waited until after nine to knock on Damien's door. When he didn't answer, she picked up the breakfast tray from the hallway table and swept inside, her cheery, "Good morning, sleepyhead..." freezing on her lips.

He was sitting up, his legs flung over the edge of the

bed, looking as if he'd tried to stand but had become dizzy. Running a hand through his hair, he peered at her. Noting her motionless form, his frown grew more curious than angry. "What's your problem?"

She swallowed. "You—you're not dressed."

He eyed her with exasperation. "The doctor helped me out of my jeans last night while you were out of the room." He tried to stand, then winced, easing back down. "Besides, you've seen me naked. Boxer shorts shouldn't bother you."

Her limbs oddly jittery, she sat his breakfast tray on the writing desk next to the door. "Well, I—I just wasn't expecting…" She let the discussion drop. Talking about his lack of attire wasn't productive. "You really should eat your breakfast in bed."

"Don't treat me like an invalid." His arm muscles bulging with the effort, he propelled himself up, his teeth clenched in discomfort. This time he succeeded in remaining upright, but only because he grabbed the headboard. "I'm getting out of here."

She stared in disbelief. "No, you're not, Mr. Lord! That mansion is a death trap. Besides, Doc Holly said you needed bed rest for at least a couple of days. And good food."

He squinted at her. "*You* added that last part, didn't you?"

Even as ill as he was, he seemed too massive for the room. She shifted her gaze to the window. All that taut, male flesh made her nervous. "Please," she whispered tightly. "Get back into bed."

"Where's my cane?"

"I don't know."

"Like hell, you don't."

She heard pain in his voice, and her gaze rocketed to

his face, the effort of his exertion etched on his features. She felt helpless, wanting to make everything better for him, but not knowing how. Her inadequacy made her mad. ''I've never seen any man or beast as stubborn as you!'' Needing to act, to do something—*anything*—she marched up to him and shoved at his chest. ''Get back into that bed!''

Taken off guard, Damien fell to the mattress. Her patience at an end, she advanced until she was standing over him, her legs between his knees. ''Don't mess with me anymore, Mr. Lord. I'm going to help you get better if I have to kill you.''

He stared up at her, looking more startled than angry. A long time passed in total quiet, but for the ticking of a bedside clock. She scowled determinedly down at him as he watched her face. He didn't move, didn't argue, and that surprised her. Still, what surprised her even more was that after a while, a silver sparkle lurked in his gaze, and she couldn't fathom why.

His lips quirked in a strange grin as his knees nudged the outside of her thighs. ''Just what kind of therapy are we talking about?''

The suggestiveness in his question was unmistakable. Her eyes widened at the intimate stroke of his skin against hers and she gasped, stumbling away from his touch.

Pointing a finger at him, she wagged it until she could form words. ''That—that was contemptible!''

He pushed himself up to one elbow, his grin ripe with soft menace. ''So was hiding my cane.''

She felt the slap of his accusation. ''Okay, maybe I lied about not knowing where it is. But if I get it for you, you have to promise you won't leave this inn.''

He snorted out a laugh. ''Sure, kid.''

She took a step toward him, then thought better of it. Her pulse rate wasn't back to normal from the last time she'd made that mistake. "If you try to leave, I'll call Doc Holly and he'll put you in the hospital. Then you know what will happen."

His expression closed at her warning, and she knew she'd pushed the right button again. "Promise you won't leave?"

His exhale was a profanity. "Okay, Miss Marquis De Sade." He took hold of the headboard and pulled himself up. "Now, may I have my cane. I'd like to wash up."

Realizing the man had to have a little freedom, she went to the closet and retrieved it. She noticed that his jeans and shirt were hanging there, too. The shirt had blood on it. Making a quick decision, she grabbed both pieces. "I—I'll wash these." At least without clothes he couldn't leave.

When she handed him his cane, she avoided eye contact. "Don't forget to eat your breakfast—"

"In bed, I know," he said, cutting in. "Now, unless you intend to give me a sponge bath, I'd suggest you leave."

She had a bad feeling he was chuckling as she made her escape. Once outside his room, she slumped against the door. Pressing a hand to her chest, she forced deep breaths, working to regain her calm. What was the matter with her? She felt tingly and light-headed.

She decided her emotional tempest was due to Mr. Lord's near nudity. Any normal woman would notice. That was perfectly understandable. And she supposed the way he'd teased her with that suggestive remark had added fuel to her agitation. Then, there was the familiar way he'd touched her...

She looked down at herself, wishing she'd worn slacks instead of cutoff jeans. She had to admit, the way his legs rubbed against hers had made her feel—different. She pressed her lips together to stifle a small, unhappy sound.

She supposed she deserved what she'd gotten, lying to him about his cane, then shoving him the way she had. Besides, a worldly man like Damien would think nothing about touching a woman with his *knees*. He'd merely been making a point. Paying her back for the lie and the shove. The brush of his flesh against hers hadn't meant a thing to him.

She pushed away from the door. Damien Lord had certainly made his point with a minimum of muss and fuss. With one fleeting caress of her legs, he not only got his darned cane back but he got a rise out of her as an amusing little bonus.

Her cat, Thalia, surprised her by rubbing against her ankle, and she jumped. She knelt to pet the cat's fluffy yellow back, embarrassed about feeling so goosey. "Just for the record, sweetie," she murmured to her purring cat, "Mr. Lord's touch didn't mean a thing to *me*, either."

It didn't.

CHAPTER FOUR

HELEN felt like a criminal, blackmailing Damien the way she had. But she knew it was for a good cause. The D'Amour mansion was in need of repairs, and wasn't a safe place for an injured man to stay. He could have broken his neck on that staircase. She closed her eyes, a painful knot forming in her stomach, fairly sure that it wouldn't have mattered to him if he had.

That's what she hated the most. Damien's lack of interest in anything—but being left alone.

She opened her eyes and resumed her climb up to his room. She had more bad news for him, and once again, it was her own doing. She knocked tentatively. "Are you decent?"

"No. I'm dancing naked on the breakfast tray."

He sounded stronger and her depression lifted in spite of his sarcasm. "Lucky I brought my camera."

When she opened the door, she saw him standing before the window, staring out at the burnished, autumn beauty of an ebbing September. Though she was far from accustomed to seeing him in his boxer shorts, she tried to keep her expression placid. He peered at her. "I've been in bed for over thirty-six hours. I'd like my pants, now."

"You've hardly been in bed at all. You've been pacing or looking out that window." She made a move to pick up his breakfast tray, but stopped herself. It was a cowardly idea, meant to get her quickly out of there. She had come on a mission, and she must not lose her nerve.

Stepping away from the writing desk, she faced him and clutched her hands together to halt their shaking. "You may have your pants. As a matter of fact, I've brought *all* your clothes to the inn. You can't stay in that big old mansion, and you know it."

His gaze flared with belligerence. "Who the hell gave you that right?"

She chewed the inside of her cheek. They both knew she didn't have any right to do what she'd done. Elissa had quoted chapter and verse of the law, complaining that she was going way out on a legal limb. Words like "breaking and entering," "theft," and "burglary" reared their ugly heads, but she stood her ground, believing she was doing what was best for him.

He shifted around, leaning heavily on his cane. "Kid, you're way out of line—"

"*I know that,*" she interrupted, conviction in her voice. "Nevertheless, it's a done deal. And if you don't like it, feel free to lump it. Remember, Elissa and Lucy and I have promised to keep your secret, but one more header down a flight of stairs could put you in a hospital—a very public situation for a man who wants privacy."

His mouth hardened. "Except from *you*, of course."

She crossed her arms before her. "If I'm going to nurse you, I have to come in and out."

"I've heard that's what kidnapper's say, too."

She huffed at him, but couldn't come up with a terse response.

"If you really are twenty-one, I hope you realize you'll be tried for abduction and looting—as an *adult*."

She was startled by the threat, but didn't believe it for one second. The last thing he wanted was notoriety. She lifted her chin. "As I've already told you, I'm twenty-one. And you're thirty-five. I weigh one hundred and twenty-two pounds, you weigh about one-eighty. I'm five feet six, you're over six feet tall. I have no weapons, and you carry a forty-four magnum *cane*. Who would believe little ol' me could kidnap big ol' you?" She smirked with self-assurance. "Besides, you don't want publicity—so let's move on, shall we?"

She searched his face for signs of softening, but found nothing. Her smile fading along with her bravado, she offered, "Okay, I understand you don't want charity. So, let's say, once you're over your headache, you can help us finish painting the parlor and the rest of the bedrooms. We won't be opening for a few weeks, so you can earn your room and board, and you can keep your precious privacy. Besides, it'll be something for you to do." She stuck her hands into her slacks pockets, her expression sheepish. "Best of all, Elissa can stop ranting at me about legal statutes I'm breaking willy-nilly."

He quirked a skeptical eyebrow. "Or I could leave town."

She frowned at the idea, but shrugged. "Of course."

His glance drifted off into the distance. After a few seconds of silence, he winced at whatever his thoughts had conjured. Helen had a feeling he realized that trying to travel incognito would be difficult for him. His face was so well-known, and his disfiguring injuries would draw a lot of unwanted attention.

Besides, traveling at all, impaired by his weakened leg, would be troublesome and painful. She sensed he was weighing his options, deciding they were few and distasteful, at best. When he turned back, bitterness twisted his mouth into a travesty of a smile. "How can I decline such a charming invitation?"

Even in the face of his mockery, she couldn't hide her

relief. "Great. I'll bring up your stuff and you can get dressed."

"You're too good to me."

His ominous scowl made her satisfied expression waver, then vanish as she plucked up his breakfast tray and fled.

"*Damien*!" Lucy gasped, her angelic face clouding with worry. "You shouldn't be up and around."

Helen had just entered the kitchen, planning to throw together some cold-cut sandwiches for lunch, only to find Damien with a bucket of paint clutched in one hand. Lucy, unaccustomed to shouting at people, was looking lost as to how to stop him.

"Point me to the parlor." His glance swung to Helen when he heard her approach. "Either of you."

Lucy gave Helen a "do something" look, but didn't speak.

Helen clenched her jaws, all too aware of how hardheaded the man could be. "I'll show you to the parlor." She waved him forward.

"But, Helen..." Lucy objected.

Helen looked at her sister, then shook her head in exasperation. "What can we do? He's a stubborn mule."

She waited for Damien to reach her. When he was at her side, she tried to take the paint from his hand, but he jerked it away. "Get your own, kid."

She slid him a complaining glance. "That's not the color we're painting the parlor, Mr. Lord." She reached for it, again. "This is Cherry Berry Blossom, for the back bedroom, upstairs. The parlor is Rhapsody in Blue. That paint's in the storage closet under the stairs."

Though his jaw worked in irritation, he let her take the can and she replaced it in the kitchen pantry, asking

Lucy to fix the sandwiches while she got Damien settled in the parlor. When she'd finished her whispered request, he was already in the entryway hall on his way to the storage closet.

She scanned him, getting a good look for the first time since he'd come downstairs. He'd taken the bandage off the cut at his temple. The area was bruised, but the inch-long gash was closed and healing. He'd shaved and was wearing clean jeans and a light green knit shirt. "You're going to paint in those?" she asked, catching up. "Don't you have any old stuff?"

Without responding, he opened the storage closet door and looked around, spotting the cans of Rhapsody in Blue. When he'd retrieved one, he turned. "These are old."

She shook her head at him, but he didn't see it, for he was heading into the reception hall that led to the parlor. "I thought you didn't know where the parlor was," she called, hurrying to reach him.

"I'm a good guesser. Besides, the dining room smelled of fresh wallpaper the night I ate dinner in there."

"Good point." She was startled by his disclosure. She'd had no idea he'd paid attention to anything that night, he'd seemed so consumed with anger.

They entered the big, airy parlor where their family furniture had been crowded into the room's center and covered with painter's tarps. Elissa looked up from her cross-legged position near the front window, her paint-brush poised above the taped-off baseboard where she'd been applying the azure color. Her expression registered surprise. "What in the world…"

Helen lifted her hands in a helpless gesture. "I know. But he won't listen to anybody. I think he's planning to make such a mess we'll beg him to leave." She turned to Damien as he set down the can, cautiously lowering himself to one knee. "Is that it, Mr. Lord? Is that your plan?" Now that she thought about it, she was only half kidding, and she hoped her expression didn't reflect her anxiety.

He looked at her, then over at Elissa. "Where did you get this little sister of yours," he asked, "Paranoids-Mart?"

Elissa reacted oddly, at first her eyes widening at his unexpected joke, then she giggled. Helen couldn't recall ever hearing her oldest sister giggle like a smitten schoolgirl. Her cheeks had even pinkened! Well, Damien Lord might not have robust health, and may have lost his chiseled, good looks, but there was no arguing that even as marred and bitter as he was, he still had a certain charisma.

Elissa looked at her sister and shook her head. "Helen's always been very trusting." She glanced back at Damien. "I, on the other hand, am not. Either she's finally taking after me, or you've had an effect on her."

He pursed his lips. "Not a positive one, I gather."

"Doesn't look that way. But that's probably for the best…she needed a reality check. Now if you'd please steal some silverware, maybe that would land her in the *real* world."

"One of those heart-on-her-sleeve types." Damien peered at the object of their conversation, his lips quirking. "Pitiful."

Elissa laughed. "Too true."

Helen didn't care to be discussed as though she were some vile specimen of fungus. "Excuse me? *Hello*!"

They glanced her way and she planted her fists on her hips. "I hate to break into your National Cynic's of

America meeting. But, just for the record, you two are *not* funny.''

Damien reached for the shoehorn they'd been using to pry off paint can lids, then looked at her, again, all teasing gone from his expression. "I won't throw Rhapsody in Blue all over the windows and floor, if that's what you're worried about."

She sniffed. "Can't you people take a joke? I was *kidding*!"

"Sure, you were, kid." The lid came off the paint with a loud squawk, then Damien picked up the stirring stick. "Let's play high stakes poker someday."

Elissa stood. "I think I'll get on the ladder and paint for a while. Helen will you hold it steady?"

Damien's glance dropped to the paint he was stirring; his expression closed. Helen could tell he was aware that they were leaving him the lower wall to paint, in deference to his injury. The flare of his nostrils made it clear that he hated being given special treatment. Here was a man who had trekked through snake-ridden swamps following risky, war-on-drugs stories, a man who leaped chasms, dodging rebel bullets. And now, this same, daring man was being given the *easiest* painting job by two pitying females. His disabled status clearly galled him.

But he said nothing, just began to brush Rhapsody in Blue above the white baseboard—their silent, grim companion.

The ringing of the phone made Helen start. Lately there was nothing unusual about that. Even sweet little Thalia rubbing against her leg could make her shriek, and Cracker's bark sent her into orbit.

"I'll get it!" Lucy vaulted from the kitchen table, where the four had gathered for a spaghetti dinner that

Helen had thrown together. "It's Stadler," she squealed as she ran through the pantry to the dining room.

When Helen's heart rate began to return to normal, she gave Elissa a look. One her oldest sister returned. Damien cleared his throat, drawing their attention. "Who's this exciting Stadler?"

Helen lowered her gaze to her plate, taking a bite and slowly chewing. She didn't care to speak against the man Lucy loved. She could hear Elissa squirm in her chair, no doubt trying to keep her opinions about Stadler Tinsley to herself, too.

Damien's chuckle drew Helen's reluctant gaze and she was instantly paralyzed. His pleasant expression, when he chose to use it, was transforming. She didn't know what had caused his slight mellowing, today, but he didn't seem as forbidding. Maybe it was the regularity of meals, or the fact that the sisters laughed and joked with each other, involving him in their lives without fanfare or hullabaloo. Or, maybe it was just the constructive activity helping keep his mind off his troubles. She had no idea. But whatever it was, her heart fluttered and sputtered at the sight of his white teeth flashing in a brief grin. "I gather this Stadler fellow you two don't want to talk about is a jerk?"

Helen fought a smile, but lost the battle. Either Damien was very perceptive or she and Elissa had less control over their facial features than she realized. "Oh, not really," she said at last. "It's just that Stadler and Lucy were supposed to get married last summer. He's a drama professor at the University of Kansas. But a couple of weeks before their June wedding, he got this chance to play the lead in Shakespeare's 'Hamlet,' so he postponed the wedding. He's touring Australia. Calls her once a week and talks about himself for ten minutes.

Lucy tries to act like the delay doesn't bother her, but...." She shrugged.

He ran a contemplative hand across his mouth. "Hmm. Lucy's a beautiful woman, and she seems like a nice person. This Stadler must not be very bright."

Helen felt a stab of something—certainly not jealousy. Lucy was as sweet and as pretty as an angel. Damien couldn't be a man and not notice. Besides, what did she care if he found other women attractive? It was none of her concern.

Elissa touched her napkin to her lips. "Well, we're assuming this acting bug is something Stadler had to get out of his system, and when he gets back in a year—"

"A year?" Damien leaned back to glance through the pantry door into the dining room, where they'd hooked up a phone for central access. Though Helen couldn't see Lucy from her vantage point across from Damien, she knew he was scanning the willowy blonde. "Stadler had better hope nobody steals her away before he gets back," he murmured almost to himself.

Helen's stomach clenched, but she didn't respond.

"Oh, if Lucy's anything, she's loyal." Elissa filled what Helen found to be an awkward silence. "She wouldn't look at another man."

"Then the guy's damned lucky." Damien turned back, directing his glance at Helen. "And speaking of lucky, that was a good dinner, kid." He revived his grin, and Helen felt it all the way to her toes. She was suddenly hot all over and feared she was blushing. His rare snatches of appreciation caught her so off guard, she couldn't move, couldn't respond.

He chuckled, glancing at Elissa. "She doesn't take compliments well, does she."

Elissa gave her sister an inquisitive glance. "Really? I hadn't noticed."

"Yes, I do!" She fought to regain herself. "It's just that you so rarely say anything nice, I wasn't expecting it."

Damien's slow grin was taunting. "And you so rarely do anything that isn't unconstitutional, I don't have much to compliment you about."

"Well, thank you very much, Mr. Lord. Remind me not to save your life the next time you dive off a flight of stairs."

Elissa lay her napkin beside her empty plate, unruffled by the squabbling. "Excuse her, Mr. Lord. She's young and hasn't learned the subtleties of good manners—like not shouting at one's guests."

Helen thought her hair would burst into flame, she was so humiliated. She would have given her sister a hard glare but the redhead had turned away.

"I'll clean up the dishes, Helen. Why don't you go somewhere and calm down. Maybe stick your head in a bucket of ice water."

Even as mortified as she was, Helen knew Elissa was reminding her not to get her emotions tangled up with Damien Lord. Unfortunately those wise, green eyes must have noticed her little sister's pinched expression while he'd rhapsodized on and on about how ravishing Lucy was. Darn that Elissa for being so intuitive. *But you're wrong this time*, her mind cried. *Really, really wrong! I'm not jealous that Damien finds Lucy to be sweet and lovely. I'm just upset because he—because you...*

She groaned, deciding she didn't dare think about the reasons she was aggravated. "I'm just fine, thanks!" Though she was yelling at both of them, she avoided eye contact, staring at the plastic, floral tablecloth. "And furthermore…"

A thought struck, and she gasped, "Oh, the *bird*!" She dashed out of the kitchen. Rushing down the stairs to the basement, she swung around the doorjamb to the right of the stairs, spilling into the laundry room.

With the noise she made entering the dark room, she heard a scraping and fluttering sound from the ventilated shoe box that was sitting on the washer. She removed the book that had been weighing down the lid, then gingerly lifted the box.

The fluttering and scratching grew louder, and she crooned, "It's okay, honey. You'll be free in a minute."

At the top of the steps, she reached for the back doorknob, but was having trouble controlling the quivering box.

"What in the hell…." Damien muttered, coming toward her.

Elissa glanced over her shoulder. Smiling wanly, she shook her head and went back to clearing the table. Helen knew Elissa's "you're a hopeless case" look quite well. But she also knew it was lovingly meant. She smiled back, remembering Elissa's gift—the necklace she now wore all the time.

Damien made it to the door before Helen could juggle the box under her arm. He grabbed the doorknob first and unlatched it. "Have you seen a psychiatrist about your hobbies?" he asked, following her onto the back stoop.

Ignoring his gibe, she walked down the four steps into the yard where branches of oaks and cottonwoods were fluttering in a crisp breeze. Holding the carton up high, she lifted the lid, and almost immediately a brown flurry of feathers merged with the sky and was gone.

"Bye," she called with a sad smile. "Be careful, Marvin."

"Marvin?" came a voice so nearby she dropped the box onto the browning grass.

She spun to see Damien staring at her with a cynical expression. "It's gratifying to see you let some creatures go."

He seemed awfully close, so she took a backward step. "If I could get *you* into a box…"

"Where do you think I am, kid?"

She didn't like the direction of the conversation, and whirled to retrieve the ventilated container. "I need to get back and help with the—"

He grasped her wrist, and his touch short-circuited her ability to speak. "So, what did the little guy do to win his freedom?"

She pulled her lips between her teeth, gathering the courage to remove herself from his grip. She yanked, and when he let her go, she found her voice. "The sparrow flew into the glass of my bedroom window this morning. I rescued it while it was stunned and helpless so my cat wouldn't kill it." Her voice climbed an octave with his towering nearness, and she cleared her throat.

He frowned. "Why bother? They're junk birds."

"No living thing is junk, Mr. Lord."

He chuckled without humor. "You've never lived in New York City."

She was startled by his quip, but didn't feel the urge to smile. He'd taken her arm again, and was aiming her toward the house. "So you name your little rescue projects?"

She didn't look at him, but scanned the branches of a nearby oak, wondering if Marvin was looking down at her in gratitude or if he was irritated at a day wasted in a box. "Yes," she admitted, when they reached the steps. "I name every creature I take care of."

"And what have you nicknamed me?" He turned her to face him. She wasn't up to meeting his derisive gaze, so she focused on his throat. Her glance was drawn to the pulse, in the hollow, there, and she had the most bizarre urge to lean forward, to lift her lips to the slow, deliberate throbbing, to touch his warm flesh with her mouth, her tongue—

"Well?" he prodded.

She winced, shocked by her turn of mind. With a shake of her head that was more of a shudder than an answer, she headed up the steps, muttering, "Pain in the neck!" She half stumbled, realizing she'd referred to the area of his body where she'd so recently wanted to place a foolish, wayward kiss.

"Do you want to hear my pet name for you?"

"*No*!" She slammed the door at her back, then found herself unable to do more than collapse against it.

A few seconds later his light knock at the glass made her cry out and drop her shoe box.

"I think Mr. Lord wants in," Elissa called from where she was washing dishes. "It's just a guess."

Lucy was drying a plate, and turned toward the commotion to see her little sister slumped against the door. "Helen, sweetie, you look flushed. Did that bird bite you?"

"I only wish it were that simple," Elissa mumbled.

Dismayed by Elissa's veiled meaning, Helen leaped away from the door as though it had become a glowing skillet. "It's not locked, Mr. Lord," she croaked, scooping up the box and heading for the basement stairs.

As she escaped to her room, she heard him come inside, heard his scraping step and the tap of his cane. But she didn't want to see him, didn't want to know his "pet name" for her—no doubt "The Kidnapping Kid" or "The Blackmailing Bully" or "Little Helen Hitler"— something nasty and sarcastic. Not that she didn't deserve it.

She slammed her bedroom door, needing to put Damien Lord out of her mind. In a few days she would go to the Chamber of Commerce dance with her true love, Hirk Boggs. Any absurd fantasies she was having about the bothersome man upstairs had to stop. *And stop immediately!*

Saturday night came on dark, swift wings—like death. Helen tried with all her heart to find the enchanting, witty qualities of Hirk Boggs's personality. After endless hours at the dance, struggling to keep a conversation going with him, she didn't know if it was her own fault or not, but she couldn't conjure up a drop of attraction for him.

Lucy and Elissa had gone to the dance, too, but without dates. Lucy, naturally wouldn't have a date, being engaged. And Elissa's whole existence, her dream, was the inn. She had no time or interest in a relationship. Still, they both knew it was their duty, as new business owners, to mix and mingle with other Branson businesspeople.

Helen hadn't been surprised that her sisters had been very nice to Hirk, though they'd both given her odd looks, as though they thought she'd gone out of her mind to accept a date with a man old enough to be her father—her not-too-bright father, at that.

Even though they hadn't voiced their doubts about the match-up, she had to agree with them. She felt *nothing* for Hirk Boggs, and by the time he brought her home, every fiber in her body was screaming to get away. Hating herself, she fibbed that she had a pounding headache and managed to avoid the dreaded good-night kiss. When she slipped into the darkened inn, she was near tears.

Both Thalia and Cracker greeted her eagerly, and their unqualified love helped. But when they'd had their fill of affection and wandered off, Helen still felt too restive to sleep.

Lucy and Elissa wouldn't be home for at least an hour. When she and Hirk had left the dance, her sisters were laughing and chatting, engrossed in a conversation with the mayor and a couple of the local show business celebrities. Yet even if they'd come home with her, she wasn't sure she could talk about it. She was too desolate even to put her feelings into words. What was she going to do? She'd tried, she really had. But—but *Hirk Boggs*! It would be like marrying the brainless scarecrow in *The Wizard of Oz*.

All was quiet and dark in the inn, and as Helen reached the basement stairs, she paused, a mewling sob escaping her throat. She knew even if sleep came, her dreams would be cruel—with Hirk drifting around in them, his toothless mouth searching out hers. She grasped the railing in disgust at the idea. Instead of descending the stairs, she twisted around, yanked and rattled the back doorknob until it reluctantly opened for her. Running down the steps, she let her tears flow freely and gave vent to her sobs.

When she reached the back gate, she threw it wide, and it banged like a bullet shot against the fence, but she didn't care. What did anything matter—a shattered fence, a bone-breaking tumble down a wooded path? Nothing could hurt her worse than the knowledge of her fate. She was doomed to a life of nonfeeling, nonlove, nonhappiness, with a bashful, eccentric simpleton.

Fresh sobs burst from her throat, so violent that she gagged and choked as she stumbled into the silent woods. The darkness was absolute, which suited her mood. Why shouldn't the atmosphere be as gloomy as her soul.

"Helen, my God," came a deep, troubled voice in the darkness.

She jerked her head up, and scanned the shadows. At first she couldn't see him, and she swiped her eyes, both in deep embarrassment that anyone had caught her in such a state, but mainly in an attempt to see. "Where— where are you?" she asked through a splintered moan.

"Here." He stepped from behind a tree and she could just make him out. Tall and lean, looking wary, his gaze raked her. "Are you hurt?"

She shook her head, but couldn't speak for trying to quell her weeping.

It stunned her when he moved close. His arm went around her, tentatively holding her as though fighting a natural reluctance to get involved. She sensed that being a comfort to sobbing women was something he didn't do often; and she had a feeling he hadn't been comforted much as a child. "Hell, that toothless boyfriend didn't try anything sick, did he?" As he spoke, his chin grazed the top of her head, and without thinking she lifted her face, nuzzling the crook of his neck, inhaling him.

He held the scent of the woods, of an autumn night, and a musky, inviting maleness that warmed her insides. Feeling lost and alone and in need of something—she didn't know what—she pressed her cheek against the pulse at the base of his throat, and closed her eyes, savoring the steady throb against her skin—like tiny kisses. Curiously her heart seemed less burdened and her soul began to rise up from the depths of Mrs. Hirk Boggs Hell.

"Helen?" he softly repeated. "What did he do?"

Though his embrace was protective and light, she became aware that he was even more solidly male than he looked. She found herself wanting to curl her arms around his chest, to pull him against her quaking body. Some willful voice inside her cried out for her to risk it, but her shyness battled the urge. She didn't dare do such a bold thing. He was merely being kind. She cleared her throat, trying her voice, for she could feel him cock his head in a questioning gesture. "He—Hirk is a very nice man." She choked out the words. "He didn't do a thing…"

For a moment there was silence between them, and Helen's world dwindled to a precious few feet. Damien's arm was gentle and caressing. His fingers were spread wide at the small of her back, comforting, compassionate. She sensed no animal lust in his actions, and felt absurd grief at that. He thought of her as a kid. That was that.

When he chuckled low, she could feel it all the way to the marrow of her bones. "So, you're sad because he *didn't* try anything?" His breath caressed her temple. "I guess that can be upsetting, too."

He loosened his hold, and she stiffened with regret. "No!" she cried, then her eyes flew open in chagrin. Had she just begged him not to let her go?

"No?" This time he released her and backed a step away. "No, what? What exactly are you upset about?"

She sucked in little, panting breaths, trying not to sway into him, to grab on for dear life. Though she could barely see his face, she knew his expression held a hint of merriment, as though he thought she was having a little-girl problem with big, bad adult sexuality. "It's not what you're thinking," she protested.

He squinted down at her in question. "What am I thinking?"

She crossed her arms before her, suddenly chilled with his body heat withdrawn. "That I'm afraid of—of a man's sexual advances. And I'm not."

He looked a little surprised, and she blanched. Oh, heavens! When would she get it through her head that he didn't think of her as a woman at all!

"You thought that's what I was thinking?"

She wished she were dead. "Uh, well…"

He shifted his cane so that he could lean his weight against a nearby tree. "Actually, I was thinking, I'm glad you're all right."

She stared at him, stunned by his unvarnished statement of caring. Her lips opened, working soundlessly until she found her wits. "You…are?"

He frowned, as though puzzled by her disbelief; then he shook his head, grunting out a self-deprecating laugh. "Right. I've been a bastard, haven't I?" His expression grew solemn. "Don't take it personally, kid. I don't hate you."

She stared wide-eyed, but she couldn't respond as her numbed mind tried to comprehend what he'd said. *He didn't hate her? Could that possibly mean he liked her?* Her heart took that leap without hesitation.

His expression changed, became watchful, and she had the horrible suspicion that some of her excitement over the possibility that he didn't hate her had shown in her face. He was disturbed by what he saw. He'd probably had to fight off amorous women all his life, and no

doubt he sensed that she might become a sighing, ador-
ing bother. And he had enough troubles.

Besides, she wanted a nice, gentle homebody type of
guy for her husband. Maybe a little more handsome and
less oddball than Hirk, but Damien Lord was the total
antithesis of her ideal husband. Being the famous, daring
sort that he was, it was obvious that he loved the rush
of danger, the adulation of thousands of women, bright
lights and action, the lack of roots. When he got better,
he'd return to that glitz and glamour world. She'd be a
fool to let her heart be stolen by such an inappropriate
man.

Unconsciously she took a defensive step away.
"Don't worry, Mr. Lord," she said sternly. "I won't
hurdle your bones." She made a face, not sure she'd
said that right. The twitch of his lips told her she probably hadn't, so she hurried on, "What I mean is, the
nature of our relationship is *not* sexual. Besides, I'm
already…" Her voice cracked at the reminder of Hirk,
the reason she'd run out here blubbering in the first
place.

He swore between clenched teeth, as though he wasn't
crazy about the fact that she needed comforting and he
was the only person around to do it. He blew out a long
breath. "What the hell happened tonight?"

She gulped down an errant whimper, rubbing her
chilly arms to create friction-warmth. "I don't want to
be any trouble."

He flicked his frustrated glance at the sky then eyed
her grimly. "Just tell me."

"Okay—okay." She looked down at her hands, noticing she was wringing them. Clasping them together,
she inhaled for courage. She had no strength left to fight.
Unable to look at him, she shifted to stare into the black-

ness of the woods. Scattered sycamores, their white bark making them look like ghost trees, were barely discernible. She focused on one. "I—I've tried to honor the fate Destiny has chosen for me, but I just can't—can't— *marry* Hirk Boggs. He…I…the only thing I feel around him is a queasy stomach." She clenched and unclenched her hands. "Besides, he keeps insisting I wear aluminum foil on my head."

Her heart pounded as she anticipated Damien's burst of laughter. A breeze ruffled dry leaves above their heads and fanned her hair. She swept a strand from her eyes, waiting. Panicking. When his chuckle came, she was prepared. Still it hurt. Closing her eyes with regret, she turned her back on him, hating the idea of his amusement.

"Aluminum foil? On your head?" His deep laugh rumbled across the night like welcome thunder after a drought. She frowned at her reaction. How dare she find his mirth at her expense even vaguely pleasant.

She shifted to scowl at him, though her heart wasn't completely in it. She thought she'd been prepared to look at him, but the sight of his broad-shouldered body lounging so near, so virile, invitingly warm in the cooling night, she felt an unwelcome stirring inside her. Angry with herself and her traitorous emotions, she spat, "I'm happy I've been so entertaining, Mr. Lord! Good night!"

She hadn't taken one step before he touched her shoulder. Though there was no insistence in the contact, she was halted as effectively as if he'd thrown an anchor around her waist. "Wait a second." The pressure of his fingers coaxed her to face him. "What is this destiny business, anyway? Were you promised to him at birth by Gypsies, or something?"

She shook her head. Forlorn, she dropped her gaze. "It's the D'Amour myth."

"You've lost me again." He planted both hands on his cane. It was obvious that he'd been standing too long and was in pain. Guilt overwhelmed her for keeping him out here. But since she'd begun this thing, she couldn't bring herself to leave, couldn't insist that he go inside for his own sake.

Though she was sure it was a waste of his time and hers, she allowed the story of the D'Amour myth to pour out. As she talked of that night, of how she'd sneaked into the mansion, and of the next morning's meeting with Hirk, she watched his face. His expression shuttered, he watched her with equal closeness. After she finished, he frowned, absorbing what she'd said. A tense minute passed before he shook his head at her. "How can you believe such horse hockey and call yourself a grown-up?"

His dismissal left her deflated. She'd known he would react that way, so it shouldn't hurt so much. "Never mind." She turned to trudge away. "Why did I think I could confide in you?"

"Hell if I know, kid."

She laughed overloud to cover the ache in her heart. "Maybe it was because you *asked*!"

When he didn't respond with something stinging and antisocial, she found herself spinning to glare at him. His lips were pursed in annoyance and she realized she'd hit a nerve. *Good!* She lifted her chin. "I won't bother you with my silly life disasters again, Mr. Lord!" she said, stomping away.

He cursed, and Helen couldn't tell if he was angry with her or with himself.

"One thing, kid," he called, his tone impatient. "You don't have your facts quite right."

His statement stilled her, and she turned back, suspicious. "What do you mean?"

"Hirk Boggs wasn't the first man you saw that morning."

As her subconscious absorbed the rest of his unspoken statement, a slow, caustic grin twisted his lips. The truth cut off her air and made her gasp. *Morning didn't necessarily mean 'after sunrise'!*

"Oh...my...heavens..." She grew unsteady and had to grab a spindly tree to remain standing. "Not—*you*..."

His wink was infuriating. "And you thought things couldn't get worse."

CHAPTER FIVE

HER SHOCKED expression seemed to have a sobering effect on him, because his grin disappeared. "Thanks, kid. I needed that ego boost." Pushing away from the tree, he approached her. "I think it's time to go inside." When he reached her, he lifted his free arm, indicating that she slip beneath it. "Care to help an old cripple to the house?"

In a daze, she unpeeled herself from the tree trunk, not sure she could support her own weight, let alone his. "But, you're not a gentle, family man. How can you be my destiny?" she asked. "I want lots of children, and I bet you don't want any."

He'd placed his arm across her shoulders, but when he heard her remark he angled his head her way. "What?" The question held a startled quality, as though he'd heard her but didn't believe it. "Children? What are you thinking?"

She looked up at his frowning face; his mouth was so near, slightly open in his shock. She ran her tongue nervously across her lips. "Well—I mean—you're a valuable human being, but you're not what I expected..."

Lifting his arm from her shoulder, he stepped back to stare. "Wait a minute." His frown became a scowl. "Just one lousy minute. I was kidding back there." He gestured with his head toward the house, and a shock of hair fell across his eyepatch. "Come on. It's late and my leg's giving me hell."

He began to move away from her, his limp more pronounced. If his head had been wrapped in a bloody bandage he'd have looked like the walking wounded from a war. Which he was, she supposed. Feeling a surge of...of...she didn't quite know what. Possibly maternal caring, or was it a need to touch him? Whichever might be the truth, it didn't matter at that moment as she scurried beneath his arm, supporting him as well as she could.

They walked through the gate into the yard, Helen's thoughts agitated. It wasn't as though the idea of marrying Damien Lord distressed her. It would simply take some adjustments in her thinking. He had been the romantic fantasy of women all over the world, and now, to find out that he was *her* destiny! It was all so new it was hard to absorb. A piercing sweetness overwhelmed her and she decided that she could possibly learn to live without children—if he *truly* didn't want them.

"Thanks for your help," he gritted, leaning more heavily against her. "I guess I overdid my exercise tonight."

She slung her arm around his trim waist, feeling pliant muscles flex beneath her palm. "You really don't believe in the myth?" she ventured, her heart pounding.

"Hell, kid, can we get off that?"

"I gather that's a no?" She didn't know how to feel. For one shining moment the adventuresome darling of millions, Damien Lord, had been her true love. At least in her mind. Probably not in any true sense. So, it was stupid to feel as though she'd lost something. Any rational person would tell her she'd never had him, so why feel—

"It's a no," he answered, cutting through her thoughts.

They reached the back steps. He lifted his arm away

from her shoulders to grab the wooden rail, then shifted to face her. "Helen." Her heart twisted at the pleasant sound of her name on his lips, spoken tenderly. Yet, she held her breath, sensing he was about to hurt her, and that he didn't want to.

"Yes?" She blinked a gathering dampness from her gaze.

He broke eye contact, releasing the banister to swipe the hair from his face. The frown that seemed to continually ride his brow, deepened. When he looked back at her, his lips were a tight line. "Marriage has never been in my plans. Besides, I've been—involved with someone for a long time."

She attempted a dry swallow. Outwardly that was her only reaction, but inside, the bottom dropped out of— something. She felt an extraordinary sense of abandonment. Not so much, his abandonment, more like the death of her naïve world view. A clammy chill settled over her heart. *So much for her childish belief in myths!*

Helen wondered if every young woman could point out the exact moment she entered adulthood. Well, unfortunately, she could. And it hadn't been on her twenty-first birthday. *This* was her growing up moment. Odd, it wasn't as pleasant an experience as she'd thought it would be. She felt as if she'd just been knocked flat.

Clearing her throat, she fashioned a smile. "I'm happy for you." The statement came out hoarsely, yet even as she said it, her numbed brain caught on the fact that he didn't seem too happy about it, himself. She had another fleeting thought. "Where is she?" It was out of her mouth before she realized she'd spoken.

Chagrin flickered across his features. Or did it? In the darkness she couldn't be positive. "Nanette leads a busy social life," he said. "She's been in Europe." Turning away, he grasped the rail for support as he pulled himself up the steps. "She's coming to visit next week."

Helen was slow to understand his last statement, uttered between clenched teeth. Once it sank in, she hurried to the top of the steps and moved to confront him. "Here? She's coming *here*?"

He mounted the last step, bringing them close, for the porch was small. "I'll let her know about the change. Unless it's a problem."

Though she felt as if she was doing something illicit, now that she knew he was involved with someone, she couldn't help but slip beneath his arm, again. "No—no, of course it's no problem. Nanette is welcome." She experienced an incongruous jealous twinge, considering the man was so totally opposite of everything she wanted in a husband. Wordlessly he accepted her support as she opened the door.

In the stillness of the house, his scent wafted around her, cool musk and subtle spices, and she wanted to run from the lush feelings elicited by his essence and the solidity of his body. But she didn't, couldn't. He needed her help all the way to his room. As they angled into the staircase hall, she forced herself to ask, "Will she be needing a room, or..." She couldn't say it. The image of Damien and his lady love-tangled in sheets— *sheets she'd bought for the inn*—took away her ability to speak.

His rueful chuckle was a surprise and she peered at his face. The glow of a lighted wall sconce next to the front door seeped into the staircase hallway, bringing his features into sharp relief. A sad smile curved his lips. "She hasn't seen me—for a while. Let's give her a little space."

So that's what's bothering him, Helen reasoned.

Damien is worried about Nanette's reaction to his scars! She was so overcome with compassion, she couldn't speak. All this time he'd been harboring a terribly human fear—the fear of being cast aside by someone he loved. His melancholy comment revealed how vulnerable he was. It seemed to say, if he lost this woman, he would disappear altogether—the Damien Lord he had known would be gone, and what remained would be the mere shell of a man.

She wanted to comfort him, reassure him, but she was too inexperienced in the ways of the world to know how to help or what to say. At the base of the staircase, she snaked her arm around his waist. Unable to trust the inadequacy of words, she squeezed gently, a sign of caring. He instantly halted, glowering down at her. "You think the minute she sees what a damned mess I am she'll dump me like everybody else has, don't you."

She was dumbfounded by his animosity and could only shake her head.

He snorted. "Sure, and you're the kid who thinks sparrows are valuable."

His constant hostility and cynicism exasperated her. Why did men—especially strong-willed men—go ballistic if they suspected the least drop of pity in a person's voice or touch? Anger rose like bile to her lips. "If Nanette dumps you it will be because you have a horrid attitude and for no other reason!" Ducking from beneath his arm, she gave him a pinched glare and poked at his chest. "I wouldn't blame her if she ran screaming back to Europe!"

She charged down the stairs, putting distance between them, her emotions a confusing muddle—anger, hurt and…and a very foolish grudging for the woman who held this man's heart in her hands.

* * *

It was strange how time seemed to have the power to stretch and condense itself at will. Even though Elissa had been busy all week interviewing cooks for the inn, and therefore the painting had gone more slowly, the days still managed to zip by as though they were fastened to an arrow, hurtling through space.

Helen watched Damien covertly as he painted, day after day, long into the night. She could see how tired he was, and that his leg hurt him, though he stood for hours, uncomplaining, brightening the walls. But the pain in his leg wasn't why he spent so much time in grim silence. She knew in her heart that he had thrown himself into painting as a means to channel nervous energy while he waited for his precious Nanette to arrive— to fill his heart or break it.

As she pulled a casserole from the oven, she heard the familiar tap-scrape sound of Damien's walk as he entered the kitchen. Dinner was almost ready. Tomorrow night at this time, Nanette would be here.

"Well, I've hired a cook!" Elissa breezed in, shucking her suit jacket and tossing it over the vinyl back of a kitchen chair. "She'll be here first thing in the morning to start getting a feel of the equipment, stocking the place with things she needs and making dishes for us to test." Helen felt her sister's enthusiastic squeeze on her shoulder as she placed the steamy, chicken dish on the table. "So, baby, you won't have to do double duty as a painter and a cook, anymore. Not that you haven't done a fantastic job."

Helen grinned, though she wasn't happy. She was as nervous as Damien for some bizarre reason, able to focus on nothing but the realization that Nanette was coming tomorrow. "How exciting, Elissa." She tried to shake thoughts of this unknown, but consequential, Nanette.

88   TO MARRY A STRANGER

"Which one did you decide on, the chatty, thin woman or the rosy-cheeked fluffy lady."

"Rosy-fluffy. Name's Bella Pizzola. She was a cook in St. Louis until her salesman-husband wanted to retire here two years ago. He died suddenly last summer, and she feels lost." Elissa's expression sobered as she repeated the woman's recent unhappiness. "She has an impeccable résumé and a need to be useful. No better references than that. I'm lucky she wants to go back to work."

"*Hooray*!" Lucy rushed from the pantry. She'd been on the phone with Stadler, and that always lifted her spirits. "Stad says he's getting rave reviews. Sounds terribly happy."

Elissa, Helen and Damien all turned in unison to look at the blonde, and with the sudden spotlight, Lucy's grin died and her cheeks grew crimson. "Oh, I didn't mean to..."

"Didn't mean to what? Talk?" Elissa teased. "Well, as long as you don't let it happen again." She motioned that Lucy take her seat. "I was just saying I hired a cook, that—"

"Bella, I bet," Lucy broke in, moving around behind Damien to take her place on his right. "She has the kindest eyes."

Elissa looked startled. "Well, yes, but I didn't hire her for her kind eyes."

Hoisting the pitcher of ice water, Lucy filled glasses all around. "*I* would have." Glancing at her older sister, she smirked. "And I'd have been right."

Helen sat down across from Damien as Elissa took her seat on his left. With a short laugh, the redhead put her napkin in her lap, and glanced knowingly at Damien. "What can I do with these two?" she asked in mock seriousness. "They're both so kindhearted it's criminal."

Damien's smiles had come few and far between this week, and Helen watched him, spellbound, when his teeth flashed in a wry expression. "I'd lock them in the cellar for their own safety."

Elissa nodded, as though taking the advice to heart. "You're a wise man."

Helen's heart did a few high-kicks at the sight of his smile—however sardonic it might be—and a chuckle bubbled in her throat. "That's not wisdom talking, the man's light-headed with hunger. Elissa, pass him the casserole."

Helen still recalled Damien's fleeting, crooked grin, as she tossed and turned, unable to sleep. She didn't know why she'd taken on his hurts and fears so personally. But she found she was as panicky about Nanette's reaction to Damien's scars as he was.

He'd told her that Nanette had visited him in the hospital right after the accident, but had left on a European trip, teeming with social obligations, before his bandages came off. It was true that he had terrible scars, and it was also true that he no longer possessed the *Gentlemen's Quarterly* cover model looks he'd once had. But, he was still the same bright, witty man he'd been. Surely Nanette would see this, surely she would cherish the fact that such a special man loved her. Surely she would appreciate his value. Surely—

Her roar of frustration split the quiet night. Helen was furious with herself for her churning thoughts. What was the matter with her? Damien's love life was none of her business. From beneath her pillow she peered at her bedside clock. *Four in the morning*. Well, beating her mat-

tress had done no good. And poor Thalia, trying to snug-
gle, had finally given up and jumped off the bed to curl
up on the rug.

Helen faced the fact that she might as well do something useful with her pent-up energies. Since cooking
helped her relax, she decided she'd take her mind off
Damien's love life and whip up a batch of Steamed Fig
Pudding—an old family favorite.

A half hour later, her mixing bowl of pudding, awash
with cloves, nutmeg, molasses and dried figs, was ready
for two and a half hours of steaming. Her mouth watered
with anticipation and her heart felt lighter. There was
nothing like creating a tasty dish to take her mind off
her problems.

As she lifted the bowl to transfer the pudding to
molds, she wondered if Nanette liked figs, then made a
face, deciding she didn't give a *fig* if she did or not.

She giggled out loud. "I don't care a *fig*, Nanette, if
you like my fig—*ooooohhh*!" Her slippered foot skid-
ded across something wet. She didn't have more than a
split second to ponder what she'd dribbled on the floor.
By the time she knew she was losing her balance, her
chin, neck and the bodice of her nightgown was sodden
with the warm, sticky mixture.

She managed to catch herself on the edge of the
counter, so the bowl and the remainder of its contents,
clattered onto the tile counter, spilling as it rolled, at last
clanking into the wall where it spun around and deposited one last dollop on her open cookbook.

She pushed herself to a stand, then just stood there.
Her features screwed up in a grimace as she plucked at
the goo. A whimper escaped her lips. "So much for fig
pudding."

Her glance darted toward the wall clock: 4:36. With

an exasperated groan, she looked down at herself. What a mess. She went to the sink and began to pick off globs of the mixture, running water to rinse it into the garbage disposal. After a few minutes she realized she wasn't making much headway. The cotton gown had to be rinsed out, and quickly, or it would be ruined.

With a disgruntled shrug, she tugged it off over her head. What difference did it make if she was only wearing panties? Nobody would be up for another hour. She might as well wash the lumpy residue out and be done with it.

She scrubbed the brownish sludge until most of the discoloration was gone, then refilled the sink with rinse water. As she turned off the faucet, she heard a noise and turned toward it.

To her horror, Damien was entering the kitchen. When their glances met, he came to an abrupt halt. His lips opened slightly and Helen saw something hot flash in his gaze.

Her heart hammering in her throat, blind humiliation choked her. With one hand fluttering up to shield her breasts from his view, she stumbled backward, grabbing instinctively for anything to cover herself—*anything*!

"Damn..." Damien's gaze raked along her body.

She grabbed at something and held it in front of her. Too late she noticed it was a tea strainer, and tossed it away, again grabbing, flailing, her gaze glued on Damien's riveted expression. "Don't—don't you..." She was only squeaking, and cleared her voice to try again. "Don't you know what you're *supposed* to do?"

He lifted his gaze, narrowed and glinting. "About now I'd be sticking a twenty-dollar bill in your G-string."

Though he was being facetious, there was an unmistakable huskiness in his voice. He wasn't taking this as lightly as he pretended. She didn't know much about men, but that look didn't suggest he was seeing the body of a "kid." And though the morning was cool, sweat had popped out on his forehead. "You're just going to stand there making jokes?" she demanded indignantly. "You're no gentleman!"

He cleared his throat. "I'm trying—but it's been a long time between..." He let the words die, clenching his teeth.

Her fingers curled around fabric, and she yanked it up to drape in front of her. It turned out to be an oven mitt, hiding little of her feminine curves. Her eyes filled with tears; she was shamed to the depths of her soul.

Damien's curse was a low growl as he limped forward. With an amazing economy of motion for a damaged man, he grabbed a fistful of the floral, plastic tablecloth and drew it sarong style around her. As it slid off the table, the wooden fruit bowl that had been the centerpiece toppled, spun, then crashed to the floor, scattering oranges and apples around their feet.

Shaky and mortified, she brushed his fingers away, but not before her skin registered his intimate heat against her flesh. Stumbling a step away, she secured the stiff plastic at her breasts with both fists and held on for dear life.

Inhaling with difficulty, her lips began to tremble. "What are you doing skulking around in the middle of the night?" she cried, trying to rationalize her lack of clothing in the kitchen.

His brows knit, but she sensed he wasn't angry, just troubled. He shook his head, his expression sincere. "I thought it was the new cook."

"Ha!" she retorted, still too upset to think straight. "And what cook would show up at *this* hour?"

As if on cue, there was a rattling at the kitchen door. Helen's glance rocketed to it and Damien turned. A grandmotherly woman, looking like a ruffled basketball and carrying a large canvas bag, was stepping inside.

She'd sat her bag down before she realized she wasn't alone. "My, goodness, I didn't—" Her pleasant greeting turned to wide-eyed alarm when she noticed Helen's lack of attire. "Lordy!" Chubby hands flew to frilly breasts. "I'm sorry. I—" She backed out, mumbling, "I'll come back in—" The door banged shut. Her canvas bag remained beside the door, an unkind, nagging reminder that it had actually happened.

When Damien faced Helen, his lips quirked. "I wonder what was wrong with her? I'm wearing sweatpants and you're in a perfectly respectable tablecloth."

She stiffened, harboring the desire to punch him in the nose for finding the situation amusing. "That's not funny. What will I tell Elissa when the cook never comes back?" Her gaze was drawn to the mocking canvas bag, and she willed it to disappear.

"She'll be back."

His chuckle grated and she pinned him with an incensed glare. A bad mistake. The man was a virile masterpiece, with the tanned, upper body of a professional athlete. His sweatpants rode low on his hips, revealing a stretch of lean belly. Flicking her disturbed gaze away, she gritted her teeth. "I hope she doesn't come back, I could never face her."

"Sure you can."

She couldn't help herself, and shifted his way, but kept her eyes elevated to chin level. "Be serious. She'll think I'm—I'm *loose*."

"So?" His grin widened, and she caught her breath. "Get a grip, Helen. This is nearly the twenty-first century, not Victorian England."

She was at a loss, her nerves tumbling and skidding. If she were to face the truth, she wasn't really that concerned about the cook. *It was Damien.* His half-naked nearness, his erotic scent, his smile, and that look—the one she'd seen in his eyes. The memory of it both disturbed and excited her.

Besides, the woman he loved was coming today. That added to—no, doubled—her turmoil. But no power on earth, no torture known to man, would get that fact out of her. Instead she summoned up the most off-putting glare in her arsenal. "I have to assume gallantry is passé in 'nearly-the-twenty-first-century,' since you're *still* hanging around, smirking at my embarrassment."

An eyebrow arched at her malicious tone. "Hey, I'd say we're even—almost." A grin curved his mouth. "You saw me naked, remember?"

She had no idea her cheeks could sizzle even more than they already did, but her face felt as if it was going to spontaneously combust.

"What were you making, anyway, kid?" He sniffed the air, seemingly unconcerned that her head was about to burst into flame. "Fig Pudding?"

She'd lost her ability to speak, and could only shrug in the affirmative. Something told her he was trying to break the tension, change the subject, treat her like a little girl, again. But it would take more than a discussion about food to do that. Possibly being swallowed whole by a gigantic Venus's-flytrap would take her mind off this fiasco, but nothing less.

His grin going playful, he bent toward her in a confiding way. She tensed but couldn't retreat. It stunned her when he didn't say anything, instead trailing his tongue along her chin. "I love fig pudding," he murmured, "and I always lick my dish."

A whisper of a gasp escaped her lips. Her eyes went wide, but that was all the movement she could muster. He hadn't touched her with his hands, hadn't yanked her lustfully against him, plunging his tongue into her ear. He'd hardly touched her at all. And, even though the impish stroke of his tongue was in no way akin to being devoured by a Venus's-flytrap, it had certainly taken her mind off the cook's expression. Unfortunately, as a side effect, the act left an unsettling impression on her heart. Now she understood the saying, "Be careful what you wish for, you might get it."

When he stepped back, he was no longer grinning and looked somehow distracted. "That wasn't a good idea, was it," he muttered.

"*You think*?" Her sarcasm was high-pitched with hysteria.

He looked at her for a second longer, before taking a step away, then bent to scoop up an apple. "I'll just take what I came for." When his gaze met hers again, Helen felt as though he was going to say something else, but he pursed his lips, apparently thinking better of it. He indicated the sink with his apple. "Do you mind?"

She shook her head, gulping several times in an attempt to quell her agitation. "Go ahead. It won't hurt the nightgown."

When he'd rinsed off the fruit and left, Helen stood there, clutching the tablecloth around her. She stared after him, burning with an invisible heat. It occurred to her that he hadn't glowered at her once, and his smiles had been sincere and perilously attractive.

And that look—that one brief glimpse she'd seen—

had radiated sensual messages so tempting she shivered with longing. This wanton side she was discovering about herself was disquieting. Her objective was to help him heal, emotionally. *That was all.* Besides, he loved someone else.

Standing there, wrapped in cold plastic, Helen made a quiet vow. She would make it a rule *never* to see Damien Lord at dawn, again. He was too sexy early in the morning for her emotions to remain totally nurturing.

CHAPTER SIX

HELEN had no idea how dreadfully long one day could be. Today had already dragged on for decades, and it was only two o'clock in the afternoon. The shipment of Buttercup Yellow paint had been delayed, so the last attic bedroom couldn't be painted. She cursed their bad luck. If the Buttercup Yellow had arrived on schedule, at least there would have been something to take her mind off the tedious tick of the clock.

If that weren't bad enough, Bella, the new cook, kept looking at her funny. Apparently the grandmotherly woman didn't take kindly to "loose" women of "nearly-the-twenty-first-century." Obviously Damien came from a world that was more casual about nudity and the wearing of plastic tablecloths than St. Louis cooks.

With Lucy and Elissa off running errands, Helen couldn't stand simply pacing around in the inn. Thalia and Cracker were settled down for afternoon naps, and didn't seem to want to be bothered. So there was little left for her to do but scream or go somewhere. *Anywhere.*

When she opened the front door, intent on a brisk walk along the shady lane that ran in front of the inn, she was startled to find Damien sitting on the porch. "Hi," he said, his expression solemn. She sensed what he was thinking. The same thing she was—Nanette would be arriving in four hours.

"Hi, yourself." She graced him with the briefest glance, still embarrassed about that morning.

"Where are you going?"

"Walk." She didn't look at him as she bounded down the front steps.

"Mind if I come along?"

She felt a jolt in her chest, trying to remain immovable on this subject. She wanted to be alone. Well, it wasn't really that, she just didn't want to be around him. He disturbed her.

She didn't hear any sounds indicating that he was rising from the chair, no creak of wood, no scrape of his cane. Apparently he was aware that she was upset about their predawn encounter, and didn't want to foist his company on her if she hated the idea. Which she did.

When she reached the bottom of the steps, she discovered she'd come to a stop. Darn her! Why couldn't she ignore the man and sprint out to the road? But she couldn't—because she knew he was suffering. She was the only one who knew how much. The fact that he'd been up so early that morning proved that he had spent his night tossing and turning, just as she had—in anxious anticipation of Nanette's arrival.

Of course he would want to do something. Just sitting, waiting, must be killing him. Her compassion flooding past her resolve to keep away from him, she turned, even managing a smile.

"Come on." There had been a wistful sound in her offer, but she decided he was a smart guy; he would know she wasn't thrilled by the prospect of his company so soon after—after...

He nodded without smiling, and pushed up from the chair. She waited for him at the bottom of the steps, but didn't watch his approach, didn't want to spend any more time looking at him than necessary. Fidgety, her gaze flitted away to scan the mid-October splendor of the Ozark mountains. Black and white hickories, black-jack oaks and sycamores blanketed the undulating land, their full, gnarled canopies fairly glowed with bright rusts and purples. Flashes of red and yellow winked amid evergreen furs.

She inhaled the briskness of the autumn day. Cool air had swept in overnight, and there was a taste of winter in the breeze. She was wearing the sweater Lucy knitted for her birthday, and pulled it closer about her.

"Cold?" he asked, very near.

She started, unaware that the day's loveliness had captured her so completely. Shaking her head, she faced him. "It's pretty here, isn't it?"

He looked around, but she couldn't tell from his closed expression if he thought it was pretty or if it was just a colorful, Midwestern prison to him.

"I smell a hickory fire somewhere," she added.

He nodded, then looked at her, unsmiling. "Where do you want to walk?"

"Along the road, I guess."

"Okay." He began to limp toward the front gate.

"You don't mind?" With two hasty steps she caught up. "What if somebody sees you?"

He chuckled derisively. "You give my supposed fame too much credit. You didn't recognize me at first, and you weren't speeding by in a car."

He had a point. "I was just thinking about you."

He peered at her, his expression wry. "Were you?"

She knew he felt her reluctance to be with him and wasn't swallowing her concern for his privacy. She shrugged. "Let's not mention this morning anymore, okay?"

"Deal." He held the gate open for her to precede him.

They walked along the shoulder of the asphalt road for a time without speaking.

"So, where's your father?"

Helen stumbled in surprise not only because of the unexpectedness of the question, but because he was expressing an interest. She turned toward him, but he couldn't see the move, for she was on his blind side. "Dad died four years ago, just before my seventeenth birthday."

He turned far enough to see her. "Sorry."

She pulled her lips between her teeth and lifted her brows in a shrug of sorts. "It wasn't sudden. He had a bad heart and sold his electrical supply business the year before, so he could take it easy."

"He left you girls the money to buy this place?"

She smiled at him, unfazed by the directness of his question. On the contrary, she was thrilled that he was showing curiosity about things. "Is this an interview?" she teased.

He pursed his lips and turned away. Her smile faded. "Sorry, again," he muttered. "Old habits..."

She felt a twinge of melancholy at the realization of how much he missed his work. "Dad left us each a little money, yes. And when Elissa decided she didn't want to practice law anymore, we pooled what we had and bought the place."

He peered at her, his expression speculative. "Elissa owes you and Lucy a lot, then."

Helen stuck her hands into her jeans pockets. "Not really. You see, it was her salary that mainly supported us after Dad died. We owed her first."

"You didn't want to use your inheritance for college?"

She looked away, growing melancholy at the memories. "Dad needed a lot of care the last year of his life. Then, after he died there were terrible medical bills. We all brought in what extra money we could. I did some baby-sitting. Lucy took in sewing. Even with the money Dad left us, there wasn't enough for luxuries like college." She shrugged. "It didn't really matter, since neither Lucy nor I felt like an advanced degree was for us. Lucy was always a whiz at working with her hands—knitting and sewing, and I—" She cut herself off. Damien already knew her lifelong dream—of a gentle husband and lots of children. She cleared her throat. "Anyway, we decided it was better to pull together and save what money we could."

He looked thoughtful and she wondered what he was thinking. Unable to help herself, she asked, "What?"

He lifted one shoulder in a half shrug. "Your family's very close. That's unusual."

She frowned. "I don't believe we're so unusual."

His mouth curved ruefully, his gaze glittering with worldly wisdom—of the cruelty, shallowness and avarice of human beings. She had a feeling he'd seen the worst of man's nature, not only in his job, but because of his injuries. Yet, rather than voice any of what he was thinking—perhaps in a desire not to taint her with his resentment—he didn't speak. He merely broke eye contact and continued walking. They lapsed into silence, and Helen could feel gloom join them on their walk, their stern companion. When she chanced to glance at Damien, she noticed his jaw working, and she knew that he had returned to brooding about Nanette.

After an interminable ten minutes, Helen's attention was diverted by a rustling in nearby underbrush. She stilled.

"What is it?" Damien's question held sharp wariness.

"I thought I saw something." She stepped further off the road.

"So what?"

She shushed him, lifting a hand in a silent request that he stay where he was.

"Helen, don't—"

She ignored his warning as the rustle came once more. This time she was sure about what she saw beneath the fronds of a hearty fern. "Aw." She squatted down. "Come on out, sweetie."

Slowly she extended her hand toward the foliage, then made a quick grab beneath the fronds.

"Helen, are you crazy?"

She turned and smiled at him as she withdrew her hand. Dangling from her fingers was a squirming, white ball of fluff, mewing and batting with baby kitten paws. "Damien," she called. "Come take it. There are two more."

She didn't hear him move so she turned, her expression pleading. "Please. I need help."

His knit brow spoke volumes. "What if they have rabies."

She made a face at him. "They can't be much over eight weeks old. I doubt that they could have anything more serious than hunger pangs." She extended the squirming kitten toward him. "Please?"

His frown intact, he limped down the rocky slope until he was beside her. Standing, she offered him the kitten.

"What am I supposed to do with that thing?"

She indicated his free hand. "Hold it against your chest. Make it feel secure."

He didn't look convinced. "What if it…?" He let the

question trail away, and it looked as though he was searching for a word.

She squinted up at him, puzzled. Then a thought came to her. "You're not thinking of the word 'poop' are you?"

His half grin was sardonic. "No, but that's close enough."

She stared at him, unbelieving, then laughed. "*This* question from a man who has done hand-to-hand combat with armed rebel soldiers?"

He examined the wriggly kitten with high disgust, but took it. "Yeah, but rebels never pooped on my shirt."

Still laughing she turned away to chase after the other two frightened kittens. She didn't know if it was for better or worse that the little things were too weak from hunger to get away. Once she had the orange-and-white one and the tortoise-colored kitten nestled to her breast, she indicated the direction of the inn. "We need to get these babies home."

"Why?" He looked skeptical. "They'd be fine out here. There are plenty of rodents and things for them to eat."

She heaved a sigh. "The idea that helpless kittens can survive when they're dumped in the wild is just a way to salve the guilt of the people who do the dumping. These babies are frail from hunger and exposure." She nuzzled the orange-and-white to her cheek. "Out here they wouldn't last another twenty-four hours. If they don't starve first, something bigger and meaner will come along and make a meal of them."

There was an unexpected reverberation against her cheek. Realizing what it was, she smiled. "He's purring." Lowering the baby against her breast again, she added, "They know we want to help them."

A questioning eyebrow arched, and it occurred to Helen that Damien had become aware of the same pleasant vibration against his chest. She inclined her head toward the kitten. "It's saying 'thank you.' Doesn't that feel nice?"

He snorted without speaking, but Helen had a feeling he wasn't quite so concerned about the prospect of being pooped on any longer.

"I was lucky." Helen carried a cup of diluted evaporated milk and an eyedropper into the second-floor bathroom. "I phoned the grocery store and caught Lucy while she was there. She said she'd pick up some strained meat."

"Sounds delicious," Damien quipped, but Helen couldn't look at him in her struggle to get inside the bathroom, barely managing to keep Thalia out.

When she finally got the door closed, she glanced at Damien. His gaze dropped from her to the kittens, huddled together on the bathroom rug. The poor dears had hardly enough strength to do more than mew weakly. He frowned at them. "Look, kid, it's your house, but why do they have to be in my bathroom?"

She settled on the cool tile floor. Placing the cup beside her, she lifted the white male into her lap. "It's far away from my room in the basement. I thought Thalia might be less curious with them up here."

She heard a pawing sound on the door and a loud meow. Clearly Damien heard it, too, for he looked at the door. "Oh, yeah, Thalia has no interest at all about what's going on in here."

She chuckled at his joke, filling the eyedropper with milk and placing it inside the kitten's mouth, but on the outside of its teeth so it wouldn't choke. She squeezed.

The kitten immediately began to lick and gulp. "Well, there was one other reason I put them up here." She indicated that he join her on the floor. "You can do the early-morning feedings."

"Oh, right."

She heard the irony in his response and looked at him, her expression going solemn. "Haven't you ever helped any defenseless little creature?"

He leaned against the pedestal sink. "Yeah, once."

Oh, Lord! He was talking about that little boy whose life he'd saved, almost at the expense of his own! She swallowed hard. Unable to hold eye contact, she busied herself refilling the eyedropper. "You didn't have pets who needed your help?"

He ran a hand through his hair. "My folks barely had time for me."

"What did they do?"

"Dad was an architect. Mother was an oral surgeon. They're retired now."

She watched as the kitten fed, still unable to look at him. "Sounds like a pretty success-oriented family."

"You think?"

His tone was so sarcastic, she glanced up. "Okay, then." She indicated that he join her again. "If you're so success oriented, help these babies live."

His features were dubious. "You forget. I'm the reporter. I don't get involved."

She glanced at her little charge. His lapping had slowed, and he seemed sated, so she decided to place him beside his white-and-orange brother and take up the tortoise-colored female. "You're involved with Nanette." She bit her tongue. Where had that thought come from?

Hearing movement, she noticed he was lowering him-

self to sit beside her. "That's hardly the same thing."
He stretched out his bad leg, laying his cane aside.

"Maybe it is the same thing, since you've said you
don't intend to get married."

He half grinned. "You're just proving my point, kid.
I don't get involved."

Her heart swelled at the sight of his grin, however
cynical, and she couldn't find her voice. To cover her
agitation, she handed him the female she'd begun to feed
and showed him how to insert the dropper. Once he'd
given the kitten a couple of eyedroppers full, she stood.
"I just remembered where another dropper is."

"You're leaving me here?"

She had her hand on the doorknob, but glanced back
at him unable to keep from smiling at the big, frowning
man cradling his tiny charge in the palm of one hand.
"If they attack, just shout. I'll come save you."

"Very funny," he grumbled as she left.

When she returned, Damien was feeding the orange-
and-white male.

"How's it going?"

"Okay. They're not dead."

She laughed and sat down beside him. "Does it
hurt?"

He looked at her. "My leg?"

"Nope." She shook her head. "Helping the helpless."

He shifted his glance to the kitten in his lap. "It's
killing me."

He was kidding and they both knew it. As Damien
fed the orange-and-white baby, she scanned his profile.
A swath of wavy hair had fallen across his eyepatch, and
a golden shaft of afternoon sun from the small window
made his hair gleam like polished jet. He was such a

massive presence in the tiny room, his musky-spicy scent compelling. Yet he seemed emotionally very far away, as though he wore his isolation like a cloak, making sure no one came too near.

She didn't believe he really wanted it that way. Possibly his parents hadn't been warm people. That was probably part of it. But, mainly he was going through a bad time in his life. And like animals in the wild, he wanted to be alone to lick his wounds. Surely he would want to rejoin, reconnect with the world, once he healed a little.

She contemplated his profile as he sat in silent concentration. She remembered his mouth from countless TV reports. It had always seemed a humorous, even kindly mouth. But rarely, now, did he exhibit any expressions other than severity or sarcasm. Still his lips were marvelous. Just full enough to be utterly masculine.

His damaged side was away from her, and her perusal lifted to his lashes. They were long, dark and curving, and seemed to brush the jutting bone of his cheek. As she stared at him, caring for his fuzzy little ward, an odd warmth began to envelop her, and a quivering welled in her core. What was this feeling? This strained anticipation, this need for—something she couldn't name?

His lips twitched slightly, and she grew puzzled. Then her glance caught on the kitten, licking his hand where a bit of milk had spilled. She experienced a tug at her insides as gentleness softened the hard lines of his face. The effect was devastating. If she'd thought he was handsome before, she was wrong. Damien was a beautiful human being, a man who was not only bright and bold and brave but someone who had tenderness and sensitivity locked up inside him.

He moved, replacing the orange-and-white kitten with

his brother and sister. "He says he's stuffed." His glance lifted to Helen. Those firm, sensual lips were *almost* smiling, and she experienced a tingle of pure delight. "What now?" He leaned slightly toward her to place the eyedropper in her palm.

His quiet nearness and the mild caress of his fingers against hers sent a tremor singing through her veins. Unexpectedly her whole being was filled with an unbearable urgency to let him know how remarkable he was. With a womanly sense of purpose, she drew up on her knees and placed a kiss on his lips.

The touch of his mouth against hers held such shocking pleasure, she buckled, and he had to catch her to keep her from falling on her face. She groaned, grabbing his neck. She hadn't meant the kiss to be more than a touch, a soft expression of her regard for him, but suddenly her wayward lips were taking no orders from her benumbed brain.

She heard a groan from deep in his throat, and she could feel him say her name against her mouth, but she didn't care that he was stunned by her impetuous act. She merely opened her lips in invitation. She understood that what she was doing was foolish, so at least some small area of her mind was still functioning. But it wasn't the part of her gray matter that got results. Just the part that could record and remember. She had a sickening sense that once this was over, she would regret it, and regret it for a very long time. But that knowledge didn't help her now.

Curling her fingers in his hair, she slanted her mouth wantonly across his, moaning with the erotic contact. He was a very big, very solid man. He could have easily thrown her off. But he didn't. He'd seemed startled, at first, even reluctant. But he'd caught her when she'd started to crumble and he'd pulled her into his lap.

She had no idea for how long she sensed his misgivings—a split second, or an eternity? But suddenly, the budding woman inside her knew that Damien was kissing her back. The warmth of his arms was manly, stimulating, and she snuggled closer as his tongue traced along her lips. His large hands moved over her back, caressing. He growled, nipping at her lower lip.

She nipped back in elated response, and their tongues danced, sweetly draining her of any virginal resistance. Now she understood what all the love songs were about. Now she knew why people died of broken hearts. "Damien..." she sighed, relishing his breath, warm and moist against her lips.

"Oh—*damn!*" he muttered roughly. Her eyes flew open at the self-reproach in his tone. For the briefest instant his lips hovered above hers before he collected himself and drew away. His gaze shimmered with heat, and she knew he'd been affected by the kiss. But she could also see that he was angry with himself. *He still thought of her as a kid.*

"Damien, please..." Her voice was so breathy she could hardly hear herself speak. "I'm a woman."

He flinched, lifting her away from his lap. His gaze smoldered but his expression had gone hard, distant. Every fiber of her body thrummed with need, but because of his sudden rebuff, she could only tremble there in a heap of humiliation, mesmerized by the conflicting emotions on his face.

Gritting out a blasphemy, he grabbed his cane and pushed himself up. "I'd better get changed."

At first his meaning didn't register, but then she remembered. Nanette would be arriving within the hour.

Dismay flooded her as she watched him retreat from the bathroom. Flinging her shaky hands to her face, she tried to stifle a sob. *Heaven spare her*! *She was falling in love with Damien Lord*! *He'd sensed it, of course—and he'd made it clear her affections were wholly unwelcome*!

Shattered by the discovery, and feeling as helpless as her furry charges, she swiped at her tears. Elissa had been right to warn her about becoming involved with a man like Damien Lord. Helen was too unschooled in the ways of the world to withstand his raging brand of charisma. She had been powerless against it, even though he had done *nothing* to tempt her.

A shiver raked her body and she hugged herself, squeezing her eyes shut. Damien was no lost dog or cat or bird. He was a man—fully functioning, sexual, and devastatingly attractive. Looking back, she faced the fact that her first instincts had been right. She should have kept on running from him as far and as fast as her legs could take her. But it was too late for that, too late for being wise or smart or even timid. She knew the man, now; and she had given him her heart—even knowing he was in love with another woman.

What a fool, what a fool, what a stupid fool she was! Somewhere in the midst of her mental chaos, Helen had one cold, lucid—and ironic—thought. It nagged at her consciousness, and no matter how hard she tried not to think about it, she couldn't get it to vanish.

Rocking back and forth on her knees, her soft keening an incongruous lullaby for the dozing kittens, she cast her teary gaze toward heaven. "Listen to me, Nanette—" A sob strangled her vow and it was a few seconds before she could go on. "May your soul be damned to the deepest pit in Hades if you break Damien's heart."

CHAPTER SEVEN

HELEN didn't know how long she sat on the chilly bathroom tiles before it occurred to her that she was monopolizing Damien's bathroom. Jumping up, she plucked a tissue from the box on a shelf above the sink. She blew her nose, then splashed water on her face.

Hearing the sound of an approaching vehicle, her heart constricted. *Nanette!* Carefully she skirted the sleeping kittens and stepped into the tub so that she could look out the window at the driveway below.

She shrank back when she saw Damien come out of his room onto the small balcony that overlooked the front yard. He'd changed into black twill trousers and a matching, knit turtleneck. Leaning forward he grasped the railing with his free hand. Helen sucked in an appreciative breath when the move emphasized the trimness of his hips. The capricious fall breeze fanned his hair and it shone like satin. Her fingers tingled to touch it, to smooth it or muss it further. It didn't matter which, as long as she could touch...

She put a trembly hand to her lips, shoving that desire aside. Unable to bring herself to turn away, her attention lingered on him, her eyes feasting, devouring every crease and ripple of his dark clothes, every wisp of windblown hair, every subtle bulge or stretch of muscle beneath fabric. Though he displayed an air of authority and self-confidence as he stood there, watching the taxi pull to a stop, Helen could see how white his knuckles had become as he gripped the rail.

The physical display of his anxiety shocked her and she suddenly couldn't stand to witness his preoccupation with another woman. She spun away, lurching from the tub. Swiping at a tear, she crouched down to look at the sleeping kittens. The sight of them there, snug and secure, consoled her battered heart, and she got herself under control. Kissing the tip of her finger she touched each fuzzy head and blessed them for their unknowing good deed.

She heard the creak of Damien's balcony door, and knew he was reentering his bedroom, on his way to greet Nanette. Since Elissa and Lucy were downstairs, already waiting, Helen didn't feel an urge to rush. Though she had to admit she was curious to see what Nanette looked like. Damien had shown her no photos nor described her in any way, and she hadn't had the nerve to ask. It wasn't until this minute that she understood why. It was because she didn't want to hear Damien's glowing recital of his ladylove's charms.

When she stood up and exited the bathroom, she was dismayed to discover her timing was supremely awkward. Damien had limped from his doorway, down the hall to the head of the stairs, and was only a few steps from her. She blinked at his unexpected nearness, but with an effort of will, managed a smile. "Uh, what's the plan?"

He grinned at her and the expression stole her breath. "Well, since Tom Cruise won't let me borrow his face, I've decided to try Plan B."

She was astonished by his offhand attitude. Her mouth worked for a few seconds before she could ask, "What's Plan B?"

"It's pretty radical," he teased. "We go downstairs."

Licking her lips, she nodded, then thought better of

it. With fidgety fingers, she smoothed her loose T-shirt over her jeans. "Oh, I'm not dressed for meeting company."

His low chuckle took her by surprise. "Reluctance? Surely not from the infamous night marauder who breaks into houses and kidnaps people." He inclined his head, his expression more serious. "Don't worry, kid. You look exactly the way Nanette will expect you to look."

Helen didn't know if that was a compliment or not and she frowned at him as he turned to lean heavily on the banister.

As he took a step down, she searched his profile for signs of tension, but saw none. The man was amazing! She'd just seen for herself how tense he was, but now there was no trace, no sign that he was nervous. He was even trying to make her feel at ease, and she'd been sure he would avoid her after she'd flung herself at him in the bathroom. She flushed miserably when she realized that he'd thought so little of her kiss that Nanette's arrival had pushed it from his mind.

When he looked back and indicated that she come with him, she moved almost as if in a trance. It was pitifully clear that she would do about anything for this man, anytime he asked.

They had made it past the first landing when a flurry below drew their attention. A striking brunette fairly erupted at the foot of the stairs. She posed there, all smiles, every long, ebony hair in place, her arms uplifted in a readied embrace.

Helen took in the fitted ruby equestrian blazer and the short, black skirt that showcased slender legs. Subtle, expensive perfume wafted up to them, and she inhaled, resenting the enchanting fragrance as much as the exquisite woman before her.

The smile on those full lips dimmed when she saw Damien, but only for a split second, before she cried, "Darling!" She wagged her fingers, and Helen noticed that her nails were long, their polish a flawless match to the blazer. "Come give Nan a hug." Helen also saw several rings that flashed costly fire, but none were on the all-important engagement finger. Of course, that meant little these days.

Elissa and Lucy appeared at the newcomer's back, their expressions polite, yet strained. Helen was struck by the realization that they were nervous about this wealthy socialite staying in an inn that reeked of paint fumes, and where most of the furnishings were covered with spattered drop cloths.

Damien laughed, a warm rich sound in the taut silence. "Who is this strange woman coming on to me?" His crooked grin was irresistible and devastating, and even though he was looking at Nanette, Helen had to grab the banister to support her wobbly knees.

The brunette's bright blue eyes widened at Damien's question, then her laughter tinkled. "Oh, you noticed my new azure contacts. I never could hide anything from you, darling. Don't you adore them? I mean gray eyes are so passé."

"I hadn't heard." Damien kidded. "Sometimes the hottest eye color bulletins come rather late to the Midwest." Elissa and Lucy laughed at his joke as he moved laboriously down the last few steps, alone. Helen couldn't get her legs to obey commands. She could only gape at Nanette—the woman who could never hide *anything* from Damien. The picture that conjured sent a pang of envy through her. And it also hurt to think the only thing she and Nanette had in common—besides their interest in Damien—was their eye color. And

Nanette had converted hers to electric blue—no doubt the *in* shade.

All of a sudden, her heart wasn't into introductions. Her heart wasn't even into beating. A shudder rushed through her when Damien reached the ground level and Nanette hugged him, kissing his unmarred cheek. "You look pale, darling," the socialite said, solicitously, then stepped away.

His grin continued to tease. "I've found a great sun block."

She shook her head at him. "*Honestly*, Damien, you're incorrigible. Don't make light of your ill health. Oh, that reminds me…" She picked a piece of lint from her jacket. "I visited your parents in their fabulous retirement home in the south of France. They asked how you were."

"Oh? And how was I?"

She'd been busily flicking the lint into the air, but with his wry question, lifted her gaze to his face. "Damien, you're such a tease," she scolded with a laugh.

There was a noise, as though a door had closed, and Nanette turned toward the sound. "Oh, cabby!" She waved in the direction of the reception hall beyond Helen's range of sight. "I'll need you to carry those to my room, dear." She turned to Elissa. "Where *is* my room, dear?"

"We've put you next to Damien, in the front corner room with the turreted bay window. It's our loveliest."

"It sounds precious." She swept her gaze back to the reception hall and the cabdriver. "Upstairs, dear."

"I don't carry bags up staircases, lady," came a gruff, winded voice. The cabby's huffing and puffing made it clear that Nanette didn't travel light, and merely getting her bags into the foyer had been drudgery.

Her pretty face fell in a pout. "Why, dear, of course you do—for a nice tip." She swept her hand toward Damien. "Can't you see the only man here isn't at all well? He can't be expected to carry my bags."

"Of course I can handle—"

"Don't be silly, darling." She interrupted him with a dismissing wave, then beamed at the cabby, again. "There's an extra twenty in it for you. Now be a precious and do it for me." Her smile was so bright, it would rival any toothpaste advertisement. Apparently the toothy solicitation worked—or maybe the twenty did it. Whichever, the portly taxi driver appeared in the staircase hall hefting two matching leather cases as he trudged toward the steps.

Helen scanned Damien's profile and thought she saw the tiniest twinge. It wasn't much of a reaction, but enough to fire her anger at Nanette's dismissal of his ability. Her insides twisted with resentment. Somehow, the harsh emotion reconnected her brain with her motor skills and allowed her to hurry down the stairs in time to get out of the glowering cabdriver's way.

Helen no longer had any desire to meet Nanette, didn't want her to exist on the face of the earth. But she *did* exist, and she was Damien's love. That was reality and she might as well get used to it. Though she was angry and feeling protective of Damien, she flung her shoulders back and marched up to the brunette, even though she knew a direct glare would display her passé eye color.

She stuck out a hand, but before she could introduce herself, Damien startled her by placing his hand on her shoulder, his thumb running along her collarbone. "Forgive me, Helen." He smiled down at her and her toes curled inside her tennis shoes. When his glance returned to Nanette, Helen's breathing had all but stopped. "Nan, this is Helen, the youngest of the Crosby sisters, and I might add, a royal pain."

He added slight pressure with his hand to emphasize that he was kidding, and his touch was sweet agony. She found it nearly impossible to remain standing as his fingers stroked along her nape. Didn't he know what he was doing to her? Growing agitated at his soft massage, she jabbed him with an elbow. "No pain, no gain, buster." He grunted in response to her blow, then laughing, released her.

Though she knew his motives had been to seem casual and jovial, it didn't change the fact that she was shaken by the contact. Inhaling, she willed her breathing to start before she keeled over in a dead faint.

Nanette, taller by several inches even if she hadn't been wearing heels, looked from Damien to Helen then back to Damien. Her regard was curious, as though she wondered, for one brief instant, if there was something between them. But quickly, her lovely lips were again smiling their assured smile. Clearly Nanette had decided she was the only woman in the room capable of attracting Damien's amorous attention. In truth, Nanette *had* seen something—unfortunately, it had been Helen's one-sided adoration.

"Oh, of course." Nanette held her soft, indifferent hand toward Helen. "Aren't you precious, Helga. You're the little girl Damien mentioned in his message." Without giving Helen a chance to correct her, Nanette fanned her lashes at Damien. "I'm sorry I wasn't at my apartment to get your call. The truth of the matter is, I stayed in Paris an extra week—I managed to get Yvonnelle to do a charity showing of his fall line. I hate to brag, but we took in over twenty thousand dollars for Yvonnelle's favorite charity.''

Damien shifted his weight on his cane. ''The home for unwed fashion designers, I presume?''

Her light laugh gurgled again. ''At least your misfortune hasn't destroyed your urbane wit, darling. And no, it had something to do with a society about erotic asphyxia.''

''For, or against?''

''You know my French is only so-so.'' Nanette waved away his question as though it hardly mattered. ''Besides, that's not the point.''

''Oh, Lord,'' Elissa mumbled.

The brunette went on with a sly smile. ''Darling, the important thing is, Yvonnelle gave me the most marvelous price on a lapis lazuli gown I've been coveting.''

Shaking his head, he gathered Nanette under his arm. ''Since the Crosby sisters have gone into understandable shock, maybe I'd better show you to your room.''

She patted the hand at her shoulder and then held on. ''I'd love that. I'm dying for a long, hot soak before dinner.''

Helen grimaced. ''Oh, Miss...'' She realized she didn't know Nanette's last name.

''She's a Bane,'' Damien supplied.

Helen was confused. ''A bane? Like to my existence?'' She bit her lip, appalled she'd said that, but luckily both Damien and Nanette laughed.

''No, precious. I'm one of the New York Banes.''

From Nanette's superior tone, Helen was sure it was supposed to be very clear, now, so she nodded obligingly. ''Oh, the *New York* Banes.'' Damien's low chuckle told her he knew her remark was a diplomatic sham.

Nanette, however, was oblivious, sweeping a strand of hair back to reveal the glitter of diamonds at her earlobe. "Yes, dear. Forgive me for my impoliteness. It's just that Damien and I have been so excited to see each other, we forgot our manners." Finally noticing Helen's worried expression, she canted her head, curious. "Is there a problem, dear?"

Helen glanced at Damien, then back at Nanette. "Uh, I, the kittens…"

Damien lifted his chin in a comprehending half nod. "She's trying to say we're housing some homeless kittens in the second-floor bathroom, and she hopes they won't be any trouble for you."

Helen swallowed, nodding. "I'm sorry, Miss Bane."

"Oh, Helen…" Elissa's tone was softly reproaching.

"We?" Nanette gave Damien a puzzled look. "You don't mean *you*, Damien? You hate cats!"

His lips quirked. "I haven't been myself."

"Of course you haven't, darling." Nanette sounded conciliatory, as though he had admitted to bouts of psychotic behavior, which she found perfectly understandable, considering his injuries. Turning to Helen, her pretty eyebrows became a puzzled line. "I must admit, dear, I'm deathly allergic to cats."

"You are?" Damien looked surprised. "I thought one of your favorite charities was The Society to Save Feral Felines."

She put a hand to her temple and closed her eyes. "True, but I don't have to share a bathroom with them. Cat hairs give me the most debilitating migraines." She eyed Helen hopefully. "Surely there are more bathrooms."

Helen caught sight of curious little Thalia strolling along behind Nanette and cleared her throat. Quickly she shifted an apologetic gaze to Elissa, who didn't look entirely pleased. "There's the one in the attic. But I can move the kittens and have the bathroom cleaned out in—"

"The penthouse! Perfect! Besides, I scatter things around a bathroom so badly, I really need one of my own." She touched Damien's arm. "Isn't that right, darling?"

Helen's chagrin over the kittens turned to heart-wrenching jealousy. Damien knew such intimate details about Miss Nanette Bane.

Elissa cleared her throat. "Well, there is one guest room up there that's furnished. But it's not nearly—"

"Don't be silly, dear. I'm sure it's precious!"

"But—but the bathroom only has a shower," Lucy added, wringing her hands.

"Shower?" Nanette made a face. "Well, it will have to do." Her expression became a beaming smile as she turned to Damien, patting his uninjured cheek. "Do you see how I sacrifice to make you comfortable, darling?"

"St. Nanette of Arc," he quipped, but there was a curious sharpness to his tone.

The brunette threw her arms out theatrically and continued as though he hadn't spoken. "Not to mention the awful trip here—two plane changes and a forty-five-mile taxi drive along twisty roads from someplace called Springfield? I mean, *really*! You had to choose the middle of nowhere to recuperate, didn't you, darling." She faced Helen again and tweaked her cheek as though she were a four-year-old. "Be a dear and run up and tell that cabby he'll need to take my bags—"

"I heard, and it'll be another twenty bucks, lady," he said between wheezes as he shuffled down the stairs.

Nanette's features grew irked. "Why that's highway robbery. Damien, tell him so!"

When the cabby reached the bottom of the stairs, Damien clasped his rounded shoulder in a comradely gesture. "We'll handle the bags from here." He drew out a twenty and handed it to the man.

When the cabdriver accepted the money, he looked up to smile at the taller man, but his grateful expression faded and his beefy face went red. "Good God, mister. You been in a bad accident or something?"

Though Helen caught her breath, Damien looked at the man, unflinching.

"Well, *really*! How rude," Nanette said. "Darling take back that man's tip!"

"Truth isn't a crime, Nan," Damien remarked quietly.

The cabdriver looked repentant and held out the money, but Damien surprised everybody by drawing out another bill. "I think you earned this." With a nod, he indicated that the cabdriver go. "And, to answer your question, yes. I was in an accident."

The place had fallen silent, and Helen wanted badly to think of something to say to change the subject, but she couldn't come up with a thing. Darn her tongue-tied bashfulness. It struck at the worst possible times.

The only sound in the room was the shuffling of the cabby's footsteps, but when he got to the foyer he stopped and turned back, looking stumped. "Hey, mister, didn't you used to be somebody?"

Nanette opened her mouth to retort, but Damien, held up a hand, effectively halting her. "That's the rumor, friend."

The cabby looked as though he had a revelation and snapped his fingers. "I know! You used to be that—that guy who ran for the state senate. That Snake Handler. Got bit in the face, huh? Bum luck.''

Damien chuckled and shrugged as though caught. ''Yeah, but you should see the snake.''

With a guffaw, the cabby turned away.

Helen's heart swelled with admiration for Damien's strength of character. She knew he was sensitive about his injuries, but you could never have sensed that from looking at him, now.

When the front door slammed shut, Nanette spun to Damien and sighed. ''Well, darling, how do I get the rest of my suitcases up to the *attic*?'' She emphasized the last word as if it was the top of Pike's Peak rather than a so-called penthouse, and Helen wondered why the woman had insisted on moving up there if she hated the idea so much. She didn't believe that *sacrifice* story for a second.

''I'll help you with your bags, love,'' Damien offered softly.

''But, you're so *ill*!''

Helen pivoted toward the reception hall, Damien's use of the word ''love'' burning a hole in her heart. ''I'll get the luggage.''

''They're a bit heavy, dear.'' Nanette sounded quite satisfied with the idea of Helen lugging her bags up two flights of stairs.

''No problem.'' She supposed she owed Elissa this little chore, considering the kitten blunder.

As she grabbed for one of the bags, a big hand brushed hers away. ''I'll get it.''

She looked up into Damien's solemn gaze. Understanding he needed to be of help, needed to prove he wasn't a helpless invalid, she nodded, astonished that he'd allowed his mask of glib charm to slip in front of her. "Miss Bane is very beautiful, Damien," she whispered, meaning it.

He hefted the suitcase and returned her smile, but there was little exuberance in it. "She's just nervous. She's really very nice." He turned away with his burden.

Helen watched him limp off and let out a wispy sigh, feeling privileged that he shared his true feelings with her. But she also felt an overwhelming sadness, knowing that he had shared so much—and would soon share much deeper intimacies—with Nanette.

"Helen, you're going to have to lock Thalia in your room." Elissa was coming down the stairs with the cat in her arms. When the redhead reached the entry to the kitchen, she thrust Thalia at her baby sister. "Miss Bane has come down with a migraine, so we can't have that cat running around spreading hair willy-nilly."

Helen clutched Thalia to her breast. "But, Elissa, Thal already feels like I don't love her since I brought the kittens home. If I lock her in the basement, she'll get depressed."

"I'm sorry and I hope the cat doesn't have to seek therapy, but—"

"Nanette isn't allergic to cats."

Both women spun toward the sound of Damien's voice. The sisters exchanged glances, then walked through the staircase hall to the reception area, where Damien was varnishing the new reception desk. "Damien, what are you doing?" Elissa asked.

He looked their way. "I thought it could use another coat."

Helen grimaced. He was so upset by Nanette's overlong lingering in her room—and now the headache—

he'd needed to find some activity to deplete his pent-up sensual energies. She swallowed hard.

"Well—well, I'm sure a fourth coat will be nice, but..." Elissa shrugged, looking at Helen. They both knew the desk didn't need varnishing. The silence pulsated with the unspoken truth about why Damien was working at something that didn't need doing. Flailing for anything to say, Helen finally asked, "What did you say a minute ago, Damien? About cats?"

He peered her way. "Nanette's not allergic to cats. She just..." He cleared his throat and removed his gaze to stroke varnish across the oak desktop. "She needs time alone to reconcile herself to—everything. I think she hoped I'd look better by now."

Helen and Elissa traded troubled glances. Could that be true? Could Nanette be making excuses not to be with him until she got used to his scars?

"Oh, no, I'm—I'm sure you're wrong," Elissa offered, and Helen was grateful, for a lump had formed in her throat and she couldn't speak.

He dipped his brush into the varnish, then lifted his gaze to Elissa and smiled. This time it was his turn to look as if he pitied someone. "It's all right. I know Nanette. She just needs time."

Thalia meowed and Helen realized she was squeezing her. She let the animal leap to freedom and scurry away. At a loss, she couldn't even look at his fine, brave face. Instead she watched the deft movements of his long fingers as he stroked along the surface.

"Helen?" Bella bustled in from the kitchen, speaking through stiff lips and narrowed eyes. There was no disguising the fact that the cook still thought of her as the "loose" sister.

Helen tried to ignore the disapproval in her tone. "Yes?"

"Lucy says there's a call for you. A Jack Gallagher."

"*Jack!*" Elissa and Helen squealed the name in unison.

As Helen ran through the pantry to get the phone, Elissa called, "Oh, I bet he just remembered your birthday. Scold him for forgetting, and tell him you'll only forgive him if he comes *personally* to visit."

Ten minutes later, Helen checked the reception hall and found it empty. She entered the kitchen as Bella was serving delicious smelling orange-tarragon chicken breasts. Helen took her usual seat on Damien's left, beaming. "Jack's in London," she announced. "And you'll be happy to know he groveled and begged my forgiveness for missing my birthday, and he said he's sending me a nice present."

"He's sending himself, I hope?" Lucy smoothed her napkin on her lap, giving Helen an expectant glance.

"It had better be him. He's been away too long." Elissa turned to the cook. "Oh, Bella, would you fix a plate and take it up to our guest, just in case she can eat?"

Bella nodded and took away the serving plate to remove a chicken breast for Nanette.

"Who's Jack?" Damien scanned Helen, his gaze discerning. "You're blushing. Another boyfriend?"

If her face had been hot before, now it was sizzling.

Elissa picked up the broccoli plate and served herself. "Jack's the first man Helen ever slept with."

Helen gasped and Lucy giggled.

"Really?" Damien tilted his head toward Elissa, but his attention remained on Helen, his glance narrowing slightly. "The first, you say?"

She lowered her gaze to her plate. Damien's watchful perusal unsettled her. "Elissa." She choked out the name. "You're a dead woman."

"Don't forget, I slept with him, too," Lucy interjected.

Damien's brows furrowed as he glanced her way. "The man must live a charmed life." He looked pointedly at Elissa. "What about you?"

She laughed. "No. I wasn't afraid of thunder."

Damien looked momentarily confused, then pretended to understand. "Ah, the fear of thunder is an aphrodisiac for two-thirds of the Crosby sisters. I must write that down."

Helen was mortified beyond words. How dare he tease them as though he cared *what* turned them on. "Jack is our *step*brother," she blurted.

He shifted toward her, his gaze intense. "I'm gratified to hear it. Incest would have been tacky."

"Oh, extremely!" Lucy's pretty blue eyes glittering with fun, she served herself a sprig of broccoli and nudged Damien's arm with the bowl to get his attention. "Before Helen has a stroke, Damien, I'd better explain. After Mother died, Dad was married to Jack's mother for a time. Jack was older than all of us, and he protected us when we were afraid. Though Dad wanted to adopt Jack, his mother objected to the idea."

Damien's dashing grin returned as he took the broccoli dish. "Ah, and he let you crawl into his bed during thunderstorms."

"Chickens that they were." Elissa teased, then added, "When Dad and Rita got divorced, we girls refused to divorce Jack. We'll love him forever."

As Damien served himself the vegetable, his glance

snagged Helen's again. "He still sounds like a lucky man to me."

Helen couldn't look at him. "He's a wonderful person."

"Why is he in London?" Damien asked no one in particular.

Lucy passed him the rice. "I bet you've eaten at Gallagher's Bistro in New York, haven't you?"

He served himself then passed the bowl to Helen. "Many times."

"Well, that's Jack's place. He's in London to open another Gallagher's Bistro over there."

Damien's eyebrows rose. "I'm impressed."

"Mr. Lord?" Bella interrupted from behind him. "The lady upstairs said this is yours." She handed him a manila envelope, three inches thick. "Said the hospital sent it to her since they didn't have a forwarding address for you."

Damien took it, but gave it hardly a glance.

"Your bill?" Helen kidded, grateful for the change of topic.

He laughed, and the rich sound did unmerciful things to her heart. "It's the right size, but no."

"What, then?"

His grin fell away and he dropped the heavy envelope on the floor beside his chair. "Just something I wrote to pass the time in the hospital."

"You wrote? Like a book?"

He frowned, shaking his head. "Hardly. Forget it."

She bent to retrieve it. "May I read—"

He grasped her wrist. "Helen, it's bad. It's nothing."

"Perfect. I have no taste at all." She didn't release the package, and kept her expression cheerful but determined. "If you let me read it, I'll handle the 5:00 a.m. feedings for Love, Honor and Cherish."

He peered at her in question. "So we've named them?"

How could she have blurted out those three words of all the words in the world? Why not Winkin', Blinkin' and Nod, or Curly, Larry and Moe? Anything but words from the marriage vows. *Where was her stupid mind*? She blanched. But even more emotionally damaging than her slip of the tongue was his touch at her wrist.

She nodded. "What—" Her voice was a quivering mess. She swallowed several times. "What do you say? I read this and you get to sleep?"

He watched her for another moment with a slow, unhurried regard that almost gave her apoplexy. When he finally liberated her from his soft grasp, he shook his head at her. "If you're that much of a glutton, be my guest."

He took up his knife and began to cut into his chicken. Helen had to forcefully snap herself out of her odd languor. It was crazy how the least contact with this man could affect her body's ability to function.

She supposed that's what love was, and the reminder stung. Even so, as she slid the envelope into her lap, she experienced a surge of elation. She might never have Damien as her true love, but he was sharing this small part of himself—this intimate look into his mind—and she felt blessed.

Sunday lunch was a quiet affair as Bella served a hearty stew to Damien and the Crosby women. The day was half over, and Nanette had yet to show herself. The sisters had spent the morning frantically finishing up the curtains for Nanette's attic room, while Damien chopped up a dead tree and stacked it for firewood. Helen had watched him from the basement workroom window as he'd labored, and knew it had been difficult for him, with his weak leg. She could tell by the way his jaws clenched and the rabid way he attacked the tree, that he was frustrated. And she didn't blame him one bit.

When he limped into the kitchen leaning heavily on his cane, Helen sat up straighter in her chair. Any room he entered immediately became charged with excitement. He seated himself, and she noticed his hair was damp from a shower, and he carried with him the clean scent of soap.

He grinned at Bella as she handed him a steamy bowl of stew, and Helen suffered a blow of heartrending tenderness over his brave front. She twisted her napkin as though it were a certain lily-white neck. How dare Nanette make him suffer this way.

As if conjuring up the object of her anger, the tall brunette whisked into the kitchen. She looked chic in an oversize beige silk sweater and linen pants. "Here's where everyone is." She breezed up behind Damien and slid her arms about his neck, leaning over to nuzzle his undamaged cheek. "Morning, darling." With a peck on his jaw she straightened, her smile fading. "Damien, you look haggard. Have you been eating?"

"Not since breakfast."

"Oh, *you*!" She flipped her hair back. "Well, I'm starving." She glanced around. "I'll just drag up a chair and sit beside you."

He had already stood. "Take mine, Nanette."

"Don't be silly. You rest." She peered around. "I'll grab that stool."

Though Damien didn't look as though he wanted her perching on the uncomfortable stepstool, he didn't argue as she scurried to get it and then placed it at his right side, which was odd, because he'd shifted in that direction to give her room at his left. She plopped down with a breathy, "There, isn't that cozy?" forcing him to shift back to the left. He peered at her narrowly, but said nothing.

Elissa and Lucy greeted the socialite with smiles, and Elissa said, "I hope you had a good night's rest."

Nanette's face fell in a pout. "No offense to your precious inn, dear, but I tossed and turned. My headache, you know."

Elissa murmured her condolences, and Lucy lowered her dubious gaze to her stew. Helen clenched her teeth, wondering if anybody else noticed that Nanette avoided Damien's scarred side like the plague. If that wasn't immature behavior, she didn't know what was.

As Bella served her, Nanette turned to Damien. "I have the most wonderful surprise. I would have told you last night at dinner, but my headache, you know."

Damien glanced her way. "Don't tell me you've discovered a cure for split ends?"

Her bell-like laughter filled the air and she took his hand in both of hers. "No, silly, I—" She paused, frowned, turning his hand in hers. "Good, Lord, Damien. What happened?" Her shocked gaze shot to his face. "Is it a burn?"

"They're called blisters." He squeezed her fingers. "I cannot tell a lie. I chopped down a tree."

She looked aghast. "But, darling—*why*?"

"Why?" His laughter was masculine and full, and though Helen sensed it was counterfeit, to his credit, it sounded real. "Don't tell me you support a society for the prevention of cruelty to dead trees."

The brunette caught on, then shook her head at him.

"Well, well, darling, you've turned into a regular Paul Bunyan out here in this back country." Withdrawing her hand from his she asked, "Now, do you want to hear my surprise or not?"

He lifted a mocking brow. "I'm thinking."

"Oh, Damien, don't tease!" Nanette took up her spoon, using it as if it were a baton as she gestured. "You remember I met Stony Silva, the country singer, when he did that concert in Boston? Such a precious man. I hear he's won several Grammies. Anyway, he's doing a televised show here in a week, and I've managed to pull off the coup of the season." She glanced around the table in a pregnant pause, then declared grandly, "I've gotten Stony to allow me to give him an After Party for charity."

"For what sexual perversion, this time?"

She nudged Damien in feigned affront. "Will you be serious? Actually, Stony insists on the American Heart Association."

"Hell. Where are the man's priorities?"

Helen laughed at Damien's sarcasm, but with Nanette's disapproving look, she stifled it.

"I know it's last minute." Her voice was strident with zeal. "But with my connections I can get everybody who's anybody to come. Stony's agreed that the After Party should start at midnight, following his concert. And I'm sure, for a *lavish* donation from HBO, we can get the party taped for a future showing on cable."

She turned to Damien and hugged him. "I realize it will take a lot of work while I'm here, but..." She released him, grinning in his direction. "Aren't you proud of me, darling?"

"You'll never know how much, Nanette." He patted

her hand affectionately, but Helen noticed a tightening along his jawline.

Removing her fingers from his, she grazed his smooth cheek with her knuckles. "Naturally you won't want to attend. We wouldn't want you to overdo."

For a split second it all flashed in Damien's gaze— the pain, the vulnerability—but he quickly concealed his hurt beneath a cavalier facade. "And my *scars* might offend people." His remark, though softly spoken, seemed to fill the room and echo back at them from every corner. "What do you think, Nanette?"

The brunette's face clouded with unease. "Scars? Why—why, Damien, I hardly... I mean, I didn't even notice..."

"Really?" he whispered. He reached across her bowl and grasped her right hand in his, deliberately pressing her palm firmly against his disfigured cheek. "My scars are over here."

With a gasp, Nanette yanked her hand away. "Oh, darling! I—I don't want to *hurt* you."

Helen's heart twisted with helpless love. Strangling the napkin on her lap, her mind screamed, *But don't you see, Nanette! You already have!*

CHAPTER EIGHT

NANETTE'S attentions to Damien were a bizarre mix of intimacy and aloofness—flirtatious, but at arm's length. Though the last thing on earth Helen wanted was to think that he and the socialite were making love somewhere in the inn, now she wasn't sure that would have been more painful than watching Damien bravely suffer this neglect at her hands.

She watched helplessly as Nanette's guileful slights took their emotional toll. Damien didn't look as though he was getting much sleep, nevertheless, during the day he worked long and hard at anything physical he could find to do. Though he hid his feelings like a man accustomed to presenting his best face before a camera, she saw the truth in the shadow of fatigue beneath his unpatched eye.

With Nanette on the phone all the time, there had been little access to the outside world for any of the Crosby sisters. Though Helen was content to spend her days with Damien, sanding, varnishing and painting, and Lucy had busied herself with the sewing of bedspreads and curtains, Elissa was having a hard time holding her temper. She'd been trying to hire a maid all week, and the lack of phone access had made it nearly impossible for prospective applicants to call for appointments.

They'd already ordered a second phone line to be installed for the inn, but when Elissa asked that it be connected earlier than scheduled, the phone company said with Branson's phenomenal growth, new condos, hotels and homes going up all the time, a schedule-change was impossible, leaving Elissa ready to explode.

Helen hadn't thought things could get more stressful, but early Thursday morning Elissa called up to her as she and Damien were preparing the last attic bedroom walls for the Buttercup Yellow that had finally arrived. The news Elissa passed on couldn't have been more unsettling. Hirk Boggs was waiting on the front driveway.

Her groan drew Damien's attention, and he stopped spackling old picture holes, lifting a brow. "Ah, the exlover returns."

She let go of the drop cloth she'd been spreading over the floor and plunked her fists on her hips. "Do you want me to *feed* you that Spackle?"

His grin was crooked and sexy, though she didn't think he was aware of it. "Maybe later, kid." He indicated the door with his putty knife. "Right now you have an admirer waiting."

She eyed heaven and turned away, his chuckle chasing her from the room. Even in her disconcerted state, the beauty of his laughter warmed her insides. He hadn't been in the mood to *really* smile or laugh much since Nanette began her Stony Silva project. *The woman had the sensitivity of a mop handle*!

Helen took the steps two at a time, hoping the sooner she got to Hirk, the sooner it would be over. When she bounded into the staircase hall she could see Nanette at the dining-room table, which had been converted into her makeshift office.

The brunette was on the phone, smiling into space. "Of course, Harrington, darling. Only a thousand dollars to attend. You know Alexandra would rather die than miss a chance of being seen on national TV in her new Helmut Lang gown. Naturally it's being taped by

HBO!" She laughed. "If you make her miss this opportunity, she'll dismember you, silly darling! She told me herself, that unhappy ten pounds she gained just before Oscar time forced her to wear..." She stopped, smiled, nodding. "Yes, and now that she's her *precious* size six, again, I know she—" A victorious smirk curled her lips. "Then I can put you two down, darling? Marvelous." She took up a pen and scribbled on a notepad. "Saturday at midnight, the Andy Williams's Theater. Now you will persuade Marta and Thad for me? Bless you, precious, I'm marking them down as a yes." She scribbled again.

It wasn't until her electric blue glance caught on Helen staring from the staircase hall that she cocked her head. "Yes, Hildagard?" Her ingratiating smile withered as she hung up.

Helen gritted her teeth, taking a side step toward the entry hall. "Nothing—Nelda."

Nanette's brows dipped, but she didn't bother to make the correction. "Dear, as long as you're here, I'd *die* for a cup of coffee."

Helen had a testy urge to inquire, "*Is that a promise?*" But, instead, she curbed her tongue and nodded. "I'll get you one. In a minute."

"Aren't you precious." Nanette dropped her gaze to the cluttered table and began leafing through papers.

Feeling as though she were a dismissed servant, Helen whirled away. When she reached the front door, she peeked through the glass, wondering why her luck with Hirk had turned sour. She hadn't heard from him since—she frowned. Had the dance only been a week and a half ago? It seemed like years. Heaving a downhearted sigh, she went outside and hurried down the steps.

Hirk smiled, displaying his lack of teeth. "Howdy, Miss Crosby. Haven't seen you for a while."

She shook her head, embarrassed to think they were both recalling the dance. She wondered if he'd found it to be the fiasco she had. "I—I guess I'm not usually outside when you deliver the butter and eggs."

"Nope." His face was going ruddy all the way to the end of his nose. "Guess not."

She swallowed, and had to force herself not to wring her hands. "What can I do for you, Hirk?"

He shrugged his slumped shoulders. "I was wonderin' if you was busy on Saturday night? There's this concert Stony Silva's going to be giving here and I thought you might want to go."

His lisping of "Stony Silva" still dampened the air as he finished his question. It went against her nature to disappoint people, but she had no choice this time. Since Hirk wasn't her destiny, there was no point in leading him on. Besides, she'd already promised herself that Damien would *not* spend Saturday night alone.

Elissa had told her sisters that she needed to go to the party, considering the publicity it would provide for the inn, and since Lucy was a huge fan of Stony Silva's, she was excited about the show. Besides, being engaged to Stadler, so far away, Lucy didn't get out much. She had a right to some fun. So that left only Helen to make sure Damien wasn't left alone to brood in the darkness.

She managed a puny smile. "It sounds like fun, Hirk, but I already have plans." None of that was a lie. She really would have liked to see Stony Silva. She was a fan, too. But some things were simply more important than personal gratification.

His face fell. "Oh, uh, sure, no problem."

Helen saw movement and was startled to notice a

woman on a bicycle turning into their driveway. The crunch of tires on gravel caught Hirk's attention, and he turned.

The woman looked to be in her early thirties and was built like an athlete of shot-put proportions. She had boyishly short reddish-brown hair, and thick, dark-framed glasses. Wearing yellow sweats and worn jogging shoes, the woman leaped from her bike almost before it stopped. "Is this—the Crosby Inn?" she asked between pants as she set the bike's kickstand.

Helen nodded, tilting her head up at the large woman, who stood almost six feet tall.

The newcomer gave Hirk a cursory look, and polite nod, then aimed her magnified glance back at Helen. "I been trying to call, but the line's busy from morning till night."

"Yes, that's true. I'm sorry." She decided not to explain about Nanette, fearing her tone wouldn't be totally neutral. "What can we do for you?"

The woman opened a pouch behind her bicycle seat and pulled out some folded papers. "I'm here to apply for the maid's job. Got my references right here. Do I talk to you?"

Helen shook her head. "No, my older sister, Elissa, is doing the hiring." She indicated the front door. "Inside."

"Now we're gettin' someplace," the woman said. Her face split in a smile, revealing a missing incisor on the right side of her mouth. It hadn't been noticeable until she'd grinned. "Can I go on in?"

Helen was hesitant. "I'd better show you." Turning to Hirk, she lifted her hands apologetically. "I have to go."

"See ya' then, Helen. Ma'am." He nodded at her,

then touched the brim of his straw hat toward the new-comer.

The bespectacled woman gave him another brief glance, then a longer one, finally smiling his way. "Nice to meet you, fella'." She held out a broad, work-roughened hand. "The name's Julienne Amber Sweet."

"Hirk." He returned, his pleasant expression gradually returning. "Boggs." Helen noticed that the two were the same height, but Julienne probably outweighed Hirk by thirty pounds of pure muscle.

Miss Sweet shook his hand with both of hers, making him stagger a little. "Good name, Boggs. Like it. Nice to make your acquaintance. I'm new to town. Come from Sand Springs, Oklahoma. Call me Jule."

He blinked, as though not accustomed to having so much information thrown at him at once, and not sure which thing to comment on. "Thanks—uh—that's nice—uh—Jule."

"Hope I see you around, Boggs." Releasing his hand, she turned back to Helen. "Do you think your sister'll mind my outfit? I mean I ain't got a car, so I gotta dress for the bike."

Helen mounted the first step indicating that the woman follow. "I don't think—"

"Uh, hope so, too."

Both women shifted to look at Hirk, who'd finally managed to respond.

Jule grinned at him and waved, then turned back to Helen. "Cute, ain't he?"

The woman's hushed assessment was so astonishing, Helen couldn't manage an answer. Obviously beauty was in the magnified eye of the beholder.

"So, what do you think about my outfit?" Jule's expression had gone serious. "Should I have worn some-thin' more dressy?"

Helen found her voice as Hirk climbed into his truck and started the engine. "No, I'm sure that's fine, Miss Sweet."

"Jule, ma'am. Plain Jule." At the top step, she caught Helen by the arm. "Say, is that Boggs guy married?"

Helen stared at the woman, into her eager, magnified brown eyes, and shook her head, unable to keep a smile from her lips. "No, Jule, he's available."

The woman revealed her lack of incisor again, nod-ding. "I think I'll look him up in the phone book and give that boy a call."

Helen couldn't help but laugh. Clearly Jule saw hid-den, irresistible qualities in Hirk that Helen had tried, but failed, to find. "Sounds like a plan." She had a feeling if Elissa hired this big, outgoing woman, not only would the inn be immaculate, but one day, bashful, gap-toothed Hirk would benefit, too.

Fresh from the shower, Helen hurried up the basement steps, shaking out her wet hair. Her stomach growled and she was ready for dinner. She stopped short when she saw Damien coming in the back door, and her heart flip-flopped. He looked wonderful, so tall, dark, his own hair showing signs of dampness. His scent drifted around her. He smelled clean. "Hi." She hoped she didn't sound as breathless as she felt. "Take a walk to build up your appetite?"

He grinned. "A short one. It didn't need to be built up, much."

She came up the last step and joined him in the small area between the back door and the stairs. "Smells good."

He placed a friendly arm around her shoulders. "Barbecue?"

"That's my guess." The weight of his arm was welcome as they walked into the kitchen and found it empty. "I wonder where everybody is?"

"I noticed Elissa out front talking to that woman who rode the bicycle here."

"Oh, Jule? I hope Elissa likes her. I do." When Damien removed his arm from her shoulders, Helen decided she'd better do something besides sway into him, which was what she wanted to do. So she scurried to the oven and opened it a crack. "Beef ribs and baked potatoes." She straightened. "Bella's a good cook. Every one of her meals we've tested so far has been great." She let out a long breath. "I just wish she liked me more."

Damien chuckled. "My little Jezebel in a tablecloth."

Though his kidding expression made butterflies cavort in her stomach, she frowned at him. "Apparently Bella doesn't live in the same, sexually open decade you admire so much."

He limped toward her, still sporting his teasing grin. "Speaking of Bella. The other day she mentioned that she never watches television."

Helen could feel her face grow hot, but pretended ignorance. "Oh? So?"

He shrugged. "So, she would have no idea who I was, then. Right?"

Helen shrugged back. "Sounds right to me."

He gave her a speculative look, then shook his head at her. "So much for Elissa's hard-nosed business methods."

Helen couldn't help but smile sheepishly. "Okay, so you know. But we *did* promise you nobody would find out your secret. Elissa decided not to hire anybody who might have seen you on TV. We got lucky.''

He leaned against the kitchen counter looking darkly scrumptious. ''I think I'm the one that got lucky.''

Helen could only drink him in with her eyes.

''But, darling, I'm absolutely desolate!'' The familiar voice drifted in through the pantry door that stood slightly ajar. Both Helen and Damien turned toward the sound. ''I mean I'm practically held hostage here in Missouri of all desolate places on the globe! Thank God I've found a project to keep me busy or I would explode with boredom! Oh, I know there are lots of theaters here. But, but Damien—well, take my word for it, he can't be seen in public in his condition.''

Helen swallowed, peering at him. His expression had gone solemn.

''I suppose he's healing, yes.'' Nanette paused, and Helen opened her mouth but he held up a halting hand, walking to the pantry door. ''He looks dreadful, just *dreadful*. You should see him, darling. Ghastly scars. And he can hardly walk, poor man. Now don't misunderstand. I'll always care deeply for him. But he's changed, so. He's not *our* Damien any longer.''

Helen watched his face, saw hurt in his gaze. ''Damien...'' she whispered, but he touched her shoulder, signaling her to be still.

''Besides,'' Nanette went on, her voice lower, ''without his work, he simply can't maintain *our* life-style, Jarvis. I've decided I must make a clean break of it before I leave. In the long run, it's for the best not to let him dangle.'' Her sigh was theatrical. ''It's just difficult to broach the subject. I don't want to hurt him while he's so ill, but I'll admit this to you, I hate this *charade* out here in the middle of nowhere. You can't know what

it's taken out of me emotionally to keep up this pretense
for *his* sake, darling.'' There was a pause while the party
on the other end of the line spoke.

After a moment, noises of a door closing and of voices
broke the silence. ''Oh, darling, I must go. Kisses to
everybody in Venice.'' She giggled. ''Yes, *especially* the
count. See you soon.'' The receiver clicked into place,
and Helen heard the familiar snap of Nanette's heels on
the wood floor. *She was heading through the pantry,
coming in to dinner.*

She had a sudden flash of inspiration, and the pain in
Damien's gaze gave her the courage to follow through
with it. Throwing her arms around his neck, she whispered frantically, ''Kiss me back—hard!''

All the need that had been roiling inside her for days
and days burst forth, and her mouth hungrily found his.
The touch of his lips sent heady intoxication rushing
through her, making her tipsy with desire, and she clung
to him.

She could tell that she'd caught him off guard, once
again, but that realization didn't register long, for it was
quickly replaced by the thrilling sensation that one,
strong arm was moving around her, drawing her against
him. She sighed, wishing he had both arms free to hold
her, to crush her into his very being.

His kiss held a tinge of anger, and she understood
why. He had been wounded by Nanette's heartless
words. Yet gradually something more than anger blos-
somed in his kiss. There was gentleness there and—and
true affection as his lips moved against hers. Though his
mouth was firm and masculine, his kiss grew tender,
slow, drugging her senses and sending a wild heat sizzling through her veins.

Oh, heavens, what foolishness had she done! How

would she ever be able to kiss another man with enthusiasm, after this? No one on earth could make her body sing with joy and burn with passion this way. She might be young, but this was a truth she knew deep in her heart—a truth she feared would prove itself out over years and years of unsatisfying kisses, once Damien was gone.

Her melancholy moan became lost in a screeching howl. "*Well*, Damien, I see you haven't withered on the vine!" Nanette slammed the pantry door behind her to emphasize the fact that they'd been caught. "I've had a suspicion you'd found yourself a simple milkmaid to satisfy your—needs! And now I see my instincts were right!"

Though dizzy from the power of his kiss, Helen knew she had to end it. Her ploy had *not* been to stand there kissing Damien for the rest of eternity, though right now it seemed like the best idea. With great regret she snaked her arms from around his neck and spun to face the socialite, trying to look guilty. "I'm sorry, Damien, but maybe it's best that she know."

Helen slid him a sideways glance, and noticed he was watching her with narrowed eyes, looking charmingly perplexed. Slipping beneath his arm, she lifted her chin toward Nanette. "The ugly truth is, Damien and I have been having a hot affair. I think it's only right that you know." Reaching up, she patted his cheek, not aware until she did it that it was his scarred cheek. "He's a flagrant skirt chaser, but he's so sexy, I couldn't say no. You're too good to waste your time on him."

Nanette was glaring at them. "Is this true?" Her voice was low and shocked.

Helen peeked at Damien. He was giving her a thorough perusal, one brow raised, but there was something twinkling in his gaze that gave her hope. At last, his lips twitched and he shifted to look at Nanette. "What can I say? I'm slime."

"He *is*!" Helen felt great relief that he was going along. But her relief was short-lived when her glance fell on Elissa, Lucy and Bella who were standing as still as fence posts in the kitchen entrance. Oh, dear. Now if only they would go along, too. Tossing a prayer heavenward, she blurted, "But we can't help ourselves, he's so hot. Isn't that right, Lucy, Elissa?" She gave them her most potent "go with me" stare. "Hasn't he propositioned you both?" Helen telegraphed an urgent plea with her eyes.

Lucy swallowed several times, and Helen could tell her middle sister was trying hard to be helpful, but didn't know quite what she should do. "Oh, why Damien has *pinched* me over and over. I'm black-and-blue."

"We call him Mr. Libido!" Helen tossed in. "*Incorrigible*. Right Elissa?"

"Er, yes. But he's impossible to resist..." The redhead blew out her cheeks, clearly uncomfortable but struggling to conjure up something racy to say. "He's such a stud..."

"A real Don Juan," Lucy added with a weak smile and wide eyes.

"You should see what the Crosby sisters do when it thunders," Damien added, amusement tingeing his voice.

Lucy laughed, then clamped her hand over her mouth, belatedly nodding pretended agreement.

"It's twisted." Helen grimaced as though making a formidable admission.

"Maybe you could throw us a charity function, Nan—call it The Society for Lewd Aerobics," Damien suggested, and Helen had a hard time keeping a straight face.

"I *knew* it!" Bella pointed accusingly at Helen. "When I saw you wrapped in nothing but that tablecloth the other morning, standing here with that man! I knew hanky-panky was going on in this house!"

Elissa's and Lucy's gasps were almost successfully masked when Helen cried, "Damien has turned our inn into a regular Payton Place. I'd run while I could, if I were you, Nanette." She slid her arm around his waist for show, loving the solid feel of him. "We're weak, but you're strong. Be strong, Nanette. Leave him!"

The socialite blinked several times, then shook out her mane of silky hair, running her hands through it, as though trying to regain her wits. "Well—I—I must say..." She pursed her full lips and eyed Damien sharply. "If it weren't for my party I would leave this instant. But I must fulfill my social obligations." Her features pinched and petulant, she tossed her head with disdain. "But for charity, Damien, I'll be noble. I forgive you."

"Don't be noble," he said quietly. "I wouldn't recognize you."

She put a hand to her breast, her electric blue eyes going so wide Helen thought her eyeballs might tumble to the floor. "Damien, you've never spoken to me that way, before. I'm brokenhearted."

He laughed, pulling Helen more intimately beneath a possessive arm. "That would be anatomically impossible for you, Nan." He glanced at a frowning Bella and smiled at her. "Dear woman, don't look at me that way, I've had a secret crush on you for some time."

When he grinned at her, Bella grew all fluttering, her cheeks going crimson. "*Really*, Mr. Lord," she huffed, but Helen could see the plump widow was affected by his playful come-on.

"If you wouldn't mind, dear lady," he went on gently. "Please send our dinners up to my room." With a devilish wink, he added, "We'll need extra barbecue sauce—for the kinky stuff."

Once they were in the staircase hallway and out of earshot, he leaned down and whispered in her ear. "Helen, I appreciate what you did back there, but you don't have to keep rescuing me. I'm a big boy."

She peered up at him through her lashes, worry gnawing at her insides. "Can you forgive me? I was just so angry."

His lips grazed her temple like the kiss of a big brother, and she felt both exhilaration and sadness. Would he never see her as anything but a nice country kid?

When their eyes met, she was startled to see approval glittering there. The softness of his regard held her a willing captive. He rubbed her arm familiarly as they went up the steps, and fresh, hot desire rushed through her like a great wave. "I'll forgive you," he murmured, "but only if you forgive me for the kinky stuff remark."

She sank her teeth into her tongue until it hurt. She didn't *dare* tell him what she'd been thinking about that!

CHAPTER NINE

ELISSA confronted Helen the next morning in the kitchen, her green eyes flashing with outrage, her expression worried. "What did you two do in Damien's room last night for two hours?"

Helen hugged her sister, and indicated that she take a seat at the table. She grabbed Bella's hand, tugging her away from the stove. "You, too. Where's Lucy?"

"I'm here." The blonde came out of the pantry carrying a fresh sack of flour.

Helen indicated the table. "Sit. I have something to explain."

"You sure do, baby." Elissa's expression was pinched with concern.

Helen patted her clenched hand and after the other two women were seated told them why she'd said Damien was her lover. "And, to answer your question, Elissa, Damien and I played with the kittens and ate dinner during those hours. That's as kinky as it got." She looked around the table at the solemn faces. "You believe me, don't you?"

"What about the tablecloth thing?" Elissa was still frowning her lawyer frown.

"Early last Saturday morning I was going to surprise you and Lucy by making our favorite pudding. But I spilled it on myself, and thinking I was alone, I decided to wash my nightgown in the sink just as Damien walked in. Naturally, I grabbed the first thing I could find to cover myself." She knew her cheeks were flaming with the memory. "It was the most humiliating moment of my life, and I'd like to forget it. Satisfied?"

"Oh, baby…" Elissa's expression softened.

Lucy took Helen's hand. "Well, personally, I think you did the right thing last night, protecting Damien's feelings that way. I'd have done the same thing—if I'd had the nerve." She smiled shyly.

Bella's brows rose dubiously. "Hmm." She pushed up from the table. "I never did like that Bane woman. Now I know why. She's got no sense. Anybody can see Mr. Lord's a good man. Always treated me like a lady." She looked down at Helen. "I wasn't sure you were a lady, though." She finally chuckled. "What kinda pudding was it you spilled? Maybe I can fix some."

"Fig."

"I'm a whiz at fig pudding." She swept a pudgy hand in the general area of her ample bosom, swathed in a pristine, ruffled apron. "And I won't spill a drop. *I'm* a professional."

The sisters laughed at her joke, and Helen felt better. But even as their female tittering filled the kitchen, she could see a vague sadness in Elissa's eyes. It was evident that her oldest sister sensed Helen's dangerous affection for Damien, and feared for her baby sister's heart. But to her credit, Elissa said nothing. Maybe she realized it was out of her hands, and no amount of well-intended lecturing would change things. Helen's heart would just have to break when the time came for him to leave. Throughout history, broken hearts had found ways to mend, and Elissa knew her sister would have to find her own way, too. Helen blessed her for understanding.

Saturday night came and went. The evening had been gala for everyone at the inn but Damien and Helen.

Though she'd fantasized any number of romantic possibilities that might occur while everyone was gone to the Stony Silva concert and the charity party afterward, the evening had turned out to be anything but her fantasized ideal.

Damien had taken a walk, alone, then retired to his room. Helen had played with the kittens, alone, then gone to bed early. But she got little sleep. She paced or stared up at the ceiling, wishing fervently that she could find a way to lift Damien's spirits, help him mend emotionally from Nanette's rejection. But she felt powerless to give him the happiness and contentment he deserved, and racked her brain to think of a way to help—*really* help.

Sunday morning, there was no painting left to do, so Damien offered to build a fire in the parlor. Though exhausted from her restless night, Helen enthusiastically assisted, pleased about their first fire in the inn. All the drop cloths had been cleared away, and the furniture and rugs were in place. With the pleasant scent of hickory smoke and the soft flicker of the flames, the parlor held a cozy, Victorian air.

Elissa and Lucy were still in bed, since they'd been up so late. Only Damien and Helen were in the parlor. At last, alone—*together*. But not quite the way she'd fantasized.

Thalia was dozing on the rug before the fire, and Helen was curled on the couch, hemming sheers for the parlor windows. Cracker snuggled against her. On her left, in the big leather chair that had belonged to their father, Damien sat silently reading the Sunday paper.

He looked absolutely perfect there, before the fire. For the first time, Helen felt as though this place might become a home to her. Damien's quiet presence made all the difference. Forgetting her sewing, she leaned her elbow on the sofa arm and gazed at him.

With his unmarred side toward her, the angular planes of his face in repose were arresting, his dark eyelashes fanning long and low as he read. His full, male lips were firmly set as though he were in deep concentration. Her flight of fancy, of course, was that he was thinking about her. That was as silly a daydream as any person could conjure, she knew, and she stifled a sigh.

The brisk sound of high heels off in the distance warned that Nanette was coming. Pushing aside her sewing, Helen slid from the sofa and padded across the carpet to Damien's chair, whispering, "Lovers would never act this way in front of a romantic fire." She tugged the paper from his fingers and let it fall to the floor and hopped into his lap. His grunt of surprise and discomfort was low, but she overlooked it as she nibbled his earlobe. The next instant, Nanette turned into the parlor, the sound of her clicking heels abruptly halting.

"Oh…" The socialite lifted her chin with affront. "I was just going to check for my cab." She walked to the window and craned her neck, scanning the empty road. "I can't imagine what's keeping it."

Damien slipped his hand up Helen's back to her nape, tangling his fingers in her hair. His other hand spanned her waist, his touch gentle and warm. "I understand the charity party was successful, Nan," he said casually.

"Naturally, darling, *I* was running it." She went up on tiptoes to see the road better. "We took in over one hundred thousand dollars."

"You worked hard. Congratulations."

"Aren't you kind." Her tone was snide, and she still didn't turn to look at them.

"I hope your trip back is comfortable." Damien

looked and sounded unaffected by her cutting tone, but Helen was having a hard time keeping her features pleasant.

Nanette spun around, eyeing him balefully. "The trip will be hell, and you know it."

He smiled mildly. "I've always admired that about you."

Her expression grew suspicious. "What?"

"Your spunky, pioneer spirit."

She sniffed and approached them. "Did you know, Damien, that you're on *Newsweek*'s Out List this month? The public is *so* fickle." She tossed her hair, the act contemptuous. "Out of sight for a few months and everybody forgets your name. I'm dreadfully sorry, darling."

Helen's arms tightened around Damien's shoulders in growing animosity. Why did the woman insist on viciously lashing out at him? She'd wanted out of the relationship, hadn't she? Pride was a very unpredictable commodity. Helen had to bite her lip to keep from talking back.

"Yes, darling." Damien's grin was wry. "You certainly are—dreadfully sorry."

The socialite pulled herself up to her full five foot nine and opened her red lips to retort, but when Cracker jumped up, barking, her eyes grew wide with expectation. "My cab!" Hurrying from the parlor, she threw open the front door. "Where have you been?" she shouted, then the door slammed behind her and her vexed tirade was muffled.

"Goodbye, Miss Bane," Helen murmured, turning to Damien. "What do you want to bet she doesn't come back in the whole time the poor guy's dragging down her bags."

Though Nanette was gone, he continued to run his fingers through her hair. "You're right. She's made her exit. She won't be back."

The deep, resonant quality of his voice, the soft caress of his fingers, made her want to sit there, cuddling— forever.

Helen's attention was seized by the slam of the front door as the same cabby who'd brought Nanette stalked inside. He looked grudging as he headed toward the stairs.

"I wonder what she promised him?" Helen speculated aloud.

"That she'd shut up all the way back?"

Helen laughed and faced him. She still had her arms around his neck, and he still toyed with her hair. When their glances came together, their smiles faded as they both realized what they were doing. His fingers stilled. "I suppose we can quit pretending now."

She felt stabbed by the reminder that *he* was pretending. Nodding, she allowed her arms to drop from his shoulders.

"By the way." He caught her hair again and gave it a tug. "I realize I'm one of your causes, and that you throw yourself into them, but you nearly crippled me when you jumped in my lap."

His breath was warm and mellow against her lips, and she had a powerful urge to lift her mouth to his, experience again the cleverness of his lips. But how many times had she thrown herself at him, already? How many times did she intend to humiliate herself before she grew up and faced the hard truth that this man didn't get involved? Especially with simple country girls?

She had to take her wayward emotions in hand, stop fantasizing about a man who thought of her as a kid, a man who would soon be leaving. Feigning nonchalance, she tweaked his chin, as though she were a doting schoolteacher. "You're a big boy, Damien. You can take it."

His teasing grin refreshed itself, and was hard to resist. With great force of will, she slipped from his lap, but discovered she was so weak-kneed, that all she could do was sink to the rug. Luckily Thalia was there, so she began stroking her thick fur. Damien would assume her intent had been to pat the sleeping cat. *Oh, how she wished that were true*!

For the next few minutes the only sounds in the inn were the crackling of the fire and the grumblings of the cabby as he struggled up and down the stairs hauling Nanette's luggage outside. Finally the roar of an engine told them the brunette was gone.

Several more hushed moments ticked by as Helen's nerves grew raw and ragged. She hadn't heard Damien pick up his newspaper. Hadn't heard him rise from the chair. So what was he doing? Brooding about Nanette's spiteful parting words? Though she felt the heat of the fire on her face, she also felt scorched along her back, as though he were staring at her. Finally, unable to stand it, she turned. "Damien?"

His steady gaze was solemn, but he quickly manufactured a smile, and she had to calm her breathing before she could say more. "I read your manuscript. I put it back in your room, this morning." She drew up on her knees in her enthusiasm. She'd been wanting to broach the subject for days. Maybe now would be a good time, help take his mind off Nanette. "It was wonderful. You should get it published. With the wonderful writing talent you have, you don't need to be tromping around in war zones dodging bullets."

His grin died and he looked away. "Sure."

She was wounded by his scoffing tone, but she couldn't let his rebuff defeat her. Not only was Damien's novel a gripping tale, but it also held great depth, insight and flashes of his charming wit. She forged on. "Damien, you have a gift as a writer. If you want my opinion, I think your good looks and success as a reporter have been holding you back from your true calling. You have a lot to offer the world—more than simply reporting the news."

His expression hard, he stared at her for a long moment. "Helen, you're hardly objective." Grabbing his cane, he shoved himself up. "Everything you touch becomes beautiful to you. Anything you rescue is worthwhile in your mind." He opened his mouth to say something else, then shook his head. "It's a damned nice quality and you're a lovely…" He let the comment drop, his jaws bunching as though in agitation. He shifted his glare toward the parlor exit. "But you have to learn the difference between daydreams and the real world."

As she watched him limp away, he blurred before her. Anguish twisting her insides, she allowed her tears to fall, knowing he wouldn't witness them.

Damien was a remarkable man who had lost so much. *Such a tragedy.* With Nanette's rejection, he'd suffered the final break from a world he'd known and loved. No wonder he was bitter. She bowed her head as a sense of inadequacy overwhelmed her. What could she do to help him find his way, again?

The next morning, Helen was startled to find Damien sitting on the bathroom floor while the kittens lapped at a saucer of baby food and evaporated milk he must have prepared.

"I thought you weren't the type to get involved." She squatted beside him and stroked the scrawny backbone of Love, the white kitten.

When he lifted his gaze, his expression was serious. "I figure I owe you."

She scanned his face, not convinced that was the whole reason. "You know what I think, Damien?"

His brow furrowed. "I never know what you think."

She smiled at his appealing male confusion. "I think your climb down from the rarefied heights has made you a better man—more real." Noticing Love had finished breakfast and was heading her way, she took the cuddly baby into her lap.

Damien's chuckle was dark and morose. "Great. I'm a real man with no career and no future."

Her smile vanished, and she reached up to touch his face. "I believe you can do anything you want to do."

Placing his hand over hers, he removed it to her lap. "That's a nice fantasy." An admonishing tone crept into his voice. "But wait until everybody tells you you're through. Then read me that fairy tale, again." His gaze glittered with unhappiness. "Don't you understand? I'm not Damien Lord anymore, and I don't know who the hell I am."

A question had been on her mind for a long time, so she decided to ask. "What—what about plastic surgery?"

"Yeah, after six or eight operations I could *still* star in 'Phantom of the Opera.'" He snorted derisively. "Why the hell can't the public deal with media figures who are less than beautiful? What's the matter with the world that it can't accept people for what they *are* rather than how they look?"

She had no urge to argue, agreeing with him wholeheartedly. But when she didn't immediately respond, he gave her shoulders a shake. "Don't you see, Helen? I *can't* do anything I want to do. So, in the future, save your girlish fancies for your kittens and your birds and your three-legged mutt."

The way he threw off her opinion as childish nonsense made her furious. In her heart, she knew he didn't think of her as a child, any longer. He hadn't called her "kid" for days, and she was positive that yesterday in the parlor he'd almost referred to her as a woman. But, for some reason, he hadn't let himself.

Her anger seething, she returned little Love to the rug and drew up on her knees before Damien. "Once and for all, Mr. Lord," she cried, indignant. "I am not a child, and you know it!"

Though she had vowed *never* to throw herself at him again, she couldn't stand the lost look in his gaze. Placing her hands on either side of his face, she lowered her mouth to his, murmuring, "Is this how a child kisses?"

A sound much like a groan escaped his throat, but Helen couldn't fathom if it was a proclamation of regret or longing. His lips were hot, stimulating, triggering primitive yearnings unfamiliar to her. Unable to stop herself, she pressed her body against him, feeling his power as his muscles rippled with tension. She could tell that he was holding himself in check, resisting the desire to give in to his urges. But there was no holding her, no desire to do so, and she clung to him as though he were her own mortality, her reason for living.

All too soon, it was over, and bleakness enveloped her soul. With an angry growl he grasped her by the arms and set her away from him. His movements unsteady, he felt for his cane as if he were a man struck blind. When he finally located it, he struggled to stand.

His jaw was tight and his breathing rough. "Dammit, Helen," he whispered huskily. "Little girls shouldn't play with fire. Don't do that again unless you mean it."

Though stricken and dizzy, she lurched to her feet, the wild pounding of her heart painful against her ribs. "What if I told you I did mean it?"

His scowl grew troubled. "*Don't*," he ordered. "I use women as a convenience. I realize now that's all Nanette was to me. A convenience. But you…" His nostrils flared. Scanning her as she trembled before him, his perusal was blazing with reluctant passion. "Never allow yourself to be any man's convenience. You deserve as much commitment as you give, and I can't offer you that."

She was crushed by his growled rejection. How many times could the human heart be shamed before it crumbled? Tears stung her eyes, so she lowered her lashes to hide her anguish. "I was wrong." She swallowed to ease the tightness in her throat. "You're the same, shallow man you always were—dedicated to noninvolvement. You made a career on your pretty face and your nerve. How ironic that you cheerfully took all the accolades your fans poured over you when you *were* beautiful, and now you demand that the rules be changed to suit *your* purpose!"

Blinking back new tears, she glared at him. "You don't want to do the work it would take to change and grow *within* yourself. How selfish and self-seeking can one man be?" In her vehemence, she slapped at his shirtfront. "Go ahead! Take the easy way out! Run back to your superficial friends and thrill-seeking journalists you crave so much."

"I told you, I can't do that." The bitterness in his tone chilled her to the bone. "Don't you get it? I was offered an inconspicuous desk job, doing background research for other reporters. That way nobody would be upset by my monstrous face." He swallowed to control his emotions, his lips curling in a sneer of resentment. "So I quit."

Scornful laughter gurgled in her throat. "Then you *are* in trouble, aren't you, Mr. Lord. You have *nothing* and you are *nobody*! Congratulations!"

His features grew ashen, but she was fuming so much with indignation for the man she knew he could be, the man he refused to see he could be, that she couldn't worry about his shock. Nevertheless, her heart rebuked her for her brutality, cried out to take him in her arms, comfort him, kiss away the hurt she'd caused.

In desperation, she slammed out of the bathroom—fearing if she hesitated one second longer she would make a fool of herself, again—run into his arms and weep for him.

Over the next tense week, Helen slowly devised a plan to get rid of Damien. Of course, that was the last thing she really wanted. But she felt he could only be happy doing what he loved, and the only way she could think of to nudge him into action was to make him furious—badger him into leaving. She sensed that once Damien stopped licking his wounds, he would discover the strength to find himself—become the man he was meant to be—on his own terms.

In order to get her plan to work, she'd put herself in league with, of all people, Hirk Boggs. It had taken the spirited encouragement of his new girlfriend, Jule Sweet, to shove him into action. But between the two women, he finally, blushingly, agreed.

Helen wasn't sure why she thought her ploy would

work, but in her gut, she felt that tonight could be the catalyst Damien needed to get on with his life.

"Now remember, Hirk," she whispered to her timid dinner date as she led him toward the front steps. "We're pretending to be in love so that Mr. Lord will see that I'm unavailable and will get on with his life. He's just so lovesick for me, I hate to see him suffer." The lie tasted horrible on her tongue, but it was kinder to Hirk than the truth would have been.

He patted her hand that was curled around his forearm. "I can see where the man might be—be crazy for you..." he lisped. "For a long while, there, so was I."

She smiled up at him. "But now that your true love has come along, I can see you're happy."

His toothless grin broadened. "Ain't Jule a doozie?"

Helen nodded. "The dooziest."

"Did she tell ya she thinks I should get me some, er, new front teeth?"

Helen was stunned, but proud of Jule for caring enough to speak her mind. "Really?"

"Think it's an idea?"

Helen didn't know quite what to say, so she nodded to give her time to think of an answer that wouldn't hurt his feelings. "I—well, if you care for her, maybe you should think about it. Besides it might help you—eat."

He frowned in thought, nodding. "That's what she said, and she's real smart. Guess I'll think on that."

"Good idea." She lowered her voice. "Okay, Hirk. It's time to play lovey-dovey."

His face went crimson in the porchlight. "I ain't sure I know how."

"Just pretend I'm Jule."

He nodded disjointedly, his features brightening.

Helen felt a surge of hope that this thing might work after all. She blessed Jule for coming along.

Elissa and Lucy were already seated at the dining room table, having been secretly informed of the plan earlier. They'd put on their happiest smiles, for they, too, wanted Damien to find his way back into his world.

Elissa stood when Helen and Hirk entered the dining room. "Hirk, dear, would you like me to take your hat?"

He reached up, removed his straw hat and handed it to her. "Thank you, ma'am."

As Elissa deposited it on a hook in the entry, Helen whispered, "Why, Hirk, I thought—well, what about the aliens?"

He bent down to confide. "Well, Jule says they can't get at your brain inside a house. And she's real smart."

Helen stared, once again amazed at Jule's remarkable influence over this man. "She could be right about that." She smiled up at him, wondering if day by day, little by little, Jule would sweetly strong-arm him into near normalcy. Her heart swelled with tenderness at the thought. Love could do astonishing things.

When Elissa reentered the dining room she indicated the table. "Hirk, why don't you and Helen sit opposite Lucy and me. Damien should be along any second."

As if on cue, their house guest limped down the final few steps of the staircase beyond the dining-room door. Hirk helped Helen into her chair. Though her back was to the entrance, she heard Damien's cane stop tapping as he noticed their guest, and where they were eating.

"What's this? A party?" As he joined them his glance swept Helen and Hirk, noting their hands entwined on the table.

"Yes." Helen's smile was stiff and she worked at looking more natural. "I invited Hirk." She shifted, gazing lovingly at her date. "We've been on the phone a lot lately, haven't we, Hirk?"

He nodded; his gappy grin looked real. She had to give him credit. When he visualized her as Jule, his expression of adoration was flawless. "I'm more than pleased for the invite, Miss Helen." He patted her hand. "I always said I'm real fond of them Crosby ladies, 'specially my little Helen."

Damien's gaze widened slightly but only for an instant.

"Won't you sit down, Damien?" Elissa encouraged, motioning toward the head of the table. "Bella is about to serve."

Once Damien was seated, the cook bustled around, bringing in delicious smelling plates heaped with food they were testing for the inn. As usual, every morsel was mouth-watering, but Helen hardly tasted a thing. Her mind was too focused on Damien's every movement, every glance.

Once, when Hirk actually worked up the courage to lean over and smooch her cheek, she thought she saw Damien go still with a bite of dilled carrot halfway to his lips. She fabricated a coquettish giggle as Damien cleared his throat. Unfortunately people cleared their throats all the time simply because they needed clearing. That didn't necessarily mean a thing. And his face gave nothing away. He was glib and charming and witty the whole time.

"Aren't they cute?" Elissa coaxed with a thoroughly believable smile. "Do I hear wedding bells, you two?"

"I'm sure I do!" Lucy's blue eyes were as excited as any sister's might be discussing a real wedding. "When are you two setting the date?" Helen was amazed at the acting ability at that table. Academy Award winners had nothing on the Crosby family.

"Oh, I'd love a spring wedding," Helen cooed, wondering at the enamored tone of her voice. It had been a fraud, but sounded so breathlessly real. "I've always dreamed of being married in April." She'd never actually thought about any particular date for a wedding, but turned and flapped her lashes at Hirk as though it *had* to be April or she'd black out from disappointment. "What do you think—honey pie?"

His Adam's apple pumped. "Sooner the better, uh, pumpkin—uh—pie…" He flushed, apparently not prepared to come up with an endearment. But pumpkin pie seemed passable.

Damien grinned their way. "Marriage?" He gave Helen an inquisitive glance. "Isn't this sudden?"

She shrugged, touching Hirk on the arm. "Oh, Damien, you know what they say—love is like a, er, rolling rock—" she smiled gamely, trying to come up with why love might be like a rolling rock "—because sooner or later it crashes into you." She managed to keep from grimacing at the stupidity of her contrived quote, but only barely.

"Love is like a rolling rock?" He scanned her face, his features doubtful. "I've never heard that one."

She laughed as gaily as she could. "Well, you should *read* more."

"Apparently." His grin grew crooked and bothersomely appealing.

Dinner lasted forever, at least that was Helen's viewpoint. But if she'd known what was going to happen next, she would have preferred to munch on dilled carrots for the rest of her life rather than move beyond the main course.

Bella brought out a silver tray, and began to serve bowls of fig pudding. When Helen saw it, her heart sputtered and stopped. She knew Bella had promised to make it, but she'd assumed it would be sometime in the distant future. Not now! Not with Damien still here!

"Fig pudding," he murmured wryly. "I prefer mine served with a tea strainer."

Though his quiet comment had been partly covered by Lucy's and Elissa's *oohs* and *ahs* of delight over the surprise dessert, Helen heard it and her gaze rocketed to his face. He looked at her for only the briefest second, but long enough for her to see amusement twinkling in his glance. He was *teasing* her, reminding her about that horrible early-morning fiasco in the kitchen. Luckily she hadn't told anyone else about mistakenly grabbing the tea strainer *before* the tablecloth.

"Did you say you wanted some tea, Mr. Lord?" Bella asked as she handed him his bowl of pudding.

His chuckle was highly disturbing as he shook his head. "No. Never mind."

Hirk's hand tightened over Helen's. "Why, Miss, uh, honey. You're all pink! Did that last bite of carrot go down the wrong pipe?"

Helen shook her head, choking out, "No—no. I'm fine."

"Are you sure?" Damien's query was laced with humor. "You do look a little feverish."

She shot a damning gaze his way. "I've never been better."

"My mistake." His lips twitched as he directed his attention at his dessert.

Bella exited amid praise for her efforts, and Helen finally managed to breathe, however erratically. Her appetite ruined, she toyed with her pudding surreptitiously eyeing Damien. He was at ease, the life of the party, making Elissa and Lucy laugh until their sides ached with implausible stories of things he'd encountered as a news correspondent.

Hirk laughed from time to time, and patted her hand often enough to seem convincing. Helen tried to join in the merriment, but her heart wasn't in it. With Hirk's big hand brushing along hers at every opportunity, she felt heartsick—both because his touch was such a strong reminder of this fraud she'd concocted, and worse, because she wished the fingers stroking hers so gently were Damien's.

At eight-thirty, her shy date finally said he had to go, since his workday began at four. Helen hurriedly walked him to his truck.

"Do you think we need to kiss?" he spluttered in her ear.

"How's this?" She lifted up on her toes and brushed his cheek with her lips. "You were magnificent, Hirk. I don't think I need to worry anymore about suggestive advances from Mr. Lord." *She could cry, that was so true*.

He shrugged. "Hope I helped."

She patted his rough hand. "You were a prince. Now, you go call Jule and tell her good-night. And thank her for me, too."

His smile broadened. "Ain't she a great person?"

"You both are."

The shrug of his slumped shoulders was his modest answer before he climbed into his van. "Oh, Miss Helen? Jule wanted to know when she should start workin'?"

"We'll be opening in about a week, so have her give Elissa a call to find out exactly when."

"Will do, ma'am. And good luck with that grabby fella'."

With that remark, his old van rumbled off.

Sadness rushed through her. How ironic that Hirk had called Damien "grabby." That was the farthest thing from the truth, much to her dismay. As she turned to go, the utter stupidity of this sham made her laugh aloud. How on earth had she thought that pretending to be in love with Hirk would bother Damien in any way? Did she really think an imagined love affair between her and the butter and egg man would make him angry enough to leave? *Damien Lord didn't get involved*! *Where had her mind been*?

Aimlessly she wandered around to the backyard, scanning the starlit sky. It was cool, but she barely felt it. She was numb.

"What in the hell was all that about?"

At the sound of the low-pitched, familiar voice, she spun but saw nothing except shadow. When Damien stepped from the darkness that engulfed the back steps, she could only stare, too startled to speak.

"Have you lost your mind—*pumpkin pie*?"

CHAPTER TEN

IT WORKED. Damien was angry. Now, she had to keep him that way long enough to get him to leave. She pretended she didn't understand his question. "What are you talking about?"

He drew near, his expression taut, all humor gone. "What kind of a game was that, pretending you're in love with Hirk Boggs?"

She drew up as straight as she could, but he still towered over her. "It was no game, Damien. It's just that since you and I last—talked—I've had what you might call an epiphany."

"An epiphany, huh?" He squinted at her, his features skeptical. "Is that what people in the Midwest call a breakdown?"

She smirked. "Very cute. Just what's so terrible about my falling in love with Hirk Boggs? He's charming and witty and—"

"His brain's one egg short of a dozen."

She frowned. "Your opinion doesn't count."

"That was *your* opinion a few weeks ago."

She shrugged. "As I said, I've had a revelation about myself, and Hirk fits right in. I want a nice, solid husband to be the father of my children. Hirk has a good business and he's very sweet."

"Dammit! You're a bright woman, Helen. Too bright to waste your life watching him snore away his evenings in his easy chair with the latest Superman comic book on his chest!"

166

"You're a snob, Damien." She turned away, hugging herself. She was shivering. It was too cold to have this conversation out here. Or was it his enraged nearness that made her quiver so? "Not everybody has t-to be a rocket scientist to be a wonderful person—and h-husband!"

"Are you cold?"

"No!"

His arm came around her shoulders, warm and sheltering, the answer to a prayer she hadn't realized she was praying.

"Maybe you're not very bright, after all," he grumbled, rubbing her arm. "You're freezing."

"Well, you're annoying."

"Helen," he whispered, his breath caressing her cheek. "Why are you doing all this lying?"

She didn't dare look into his discerning gaze, and stiffened with resolve. "I'm not lying. I love Hirk, and I've accepted his proposal of marriage. If you don't like it, you can leave."

His arm tightened around her shoulders in a flinch of surprise. "Leave?"

She stared off into the dark woods, pulling her lips between her teeth to quell their trembling. After a moment, she nodded.

"But, Helen, as your friend, I have to tell you this guy won't make you happy."

His scent, his nearness, tormented her, but she couldn't bring herself to draw away. Reluctantly she peered up at him. "Friendship is a commitment, Damien." Her voice was harsh with feeling. "Don't go out of your way."

"Dammit!" He moved around to face her, his expression more upset than angry. "It's one thing to take in the broken castoffs of the world, but it's another thing to marry one of them.''

"Who I marry is my business."

He lifted a frustrated glance toward heaven, his groan a profanity. ''I can't stand to see you waste yourself on such a loser.''

She swallowed, drawing on all her courage. *It was now or never.* "And you know all about losers, don't you, Damien!'' The ugly slur tasted sour on her tongue, but it had to be said.

Even in the dusky light, she could see that he was broadsided by her insult. He stood there so silently, so still, searching her face. ''Is that what you think I am?'' At his hushed question a stab of guilt plunged deep into her chest, and she bled. ''You really believe I'm a loser?''

No! No, that's not what I think! she wanted to scream. *I love you! I think you could be a power in this world, if you only tried!* But she had to keep her agonized thoughts a secret and remain steadfast in her lie, so she jerked a nod. ''With our inn opening in a week we'll need your room. Besides, somebody might recognize you—you'd have to leave then, anyway, and find someplace else to *hide*.'' Her misery was so acute, it was a pulsing, physical pain, but she hid the blubbering mess she was behind a stubborn mask.

''I see.''

There was affliction in his tone, and the sound sent ice spreading through her body. A dull ache throbbed where her heart once beat. She opened her lips to add insult to injury, but suddenly couldn't bear to cause him more suffering. Snapping her lips shut, she stomped up the back steps. As she slammed into the house, her composure failed her, and she burst into brokenhearted sobs.

*   *   *

The next morning Helen yawned behind her hand, trying to hide the fact that she'd gotten no sleep last night. What had hurting Damien accomplished, after all? He hadn't said he was leaving. It was nearly ten, and so far, she hadn't seen him today. That was only because she hadn't come upstairs for breakfast, for Elissa and Lucy commented that he'd been there.

"Package for you, Helen," Elissa called, snapping her from her reverie. The redhead came in the front door carrying the mail. "It's from Jack. I bet it's the birthday present he promised you."

Helen felt a surge of happiness at the mention of their stepbrother. He was sweet to send her something, especially since he was so busy. She took the shoe-size box from Elissa's hands and carried it to the dining-room table.

"Lucy," Elissa called through the pantry. "Jack's present to Helen is here. Oh, and I have a postcard for you from Stadler." As Helen pulled off the tape that secured the box, her oldest sister confided in her ear, "Listen to this card. 'Lucy. Been busy. I'm getting rave reviews. I'll send clippings later for you to put in my scrapbook. Love, Stad.'" She wrinkled her nose. "Oh, boy. He might as well write, 'Having a wonderful time and I'm not giving you a thought except when I need a slave.'"

Helen frowned and shushed Elissa as Lucy breezed in from the pantry. "Something for me?"

Elissa thrust out the card at arm's length as though it were contagious and she feared catching something. "Lover boy strikes again."

Lucy took the card and read, her expression of excitement dying. "Well—he's fine. That's good."

"I'm thrilled," Elissa scoffed, then turned to Helen. "How are you doing? Need a knife?"

Helen ripped the last piece of tape off the box. "Got it."

She carefully opened the tissue wrappings to find a porcelain Limoges box shaped like a young woman clutching a white kitten to her breast. The figure, her legs curled beneath her on a tufted ottoman, bore a resemblance to Helen, with brown hair and gray eyes. Her skin was as translucent as a pearl. Just beneath the tufted pad of the tiny ottoman, was the beautifully crafted clasp for the box, a petite work of art in itself.

"Oh, my…" Helen breathed. "How beautiful."

"Open it," Lucy said. "Sometimes these boxes have a surprise inside."

Helen unlocked the clasp and gasped in awe when she saw that inside the box was another white kitten, curled up sleeping. "Oh, he shouldn't have done this," she cried. "It's too expensive."

"But it's perfect." Elissa beamed at her sister. "It's you."

Helen smiled, gazing down at the diminutive collector's item in her hand. Her heart would have been bursting with excitement if her mind hadn't been so full of memories of Damien's afflicted expression last night. Trying again to shake off the vision, she sighed. "Well, I vote Jack as my favorite man in the world."

"Oh, look." Elissa held up an envelope. "Here's a note."

Helen closed the box and placed it on the table. She opened the note and read aloud. "Helen. You're a grown-up woman, now. Save me a kiss. Jack." She smiled, but there was melancholy in it. At least Jack thought of her as a woman.

A noise attracted their attention and the sisters turned to see Damien on the bottom step of the stairs, a suitcase in his hand. He looked terribly handsome, and new anguish seared her heart. Jack's note slipped from her fingers when their solemn gazes clashed. She wondered how long he had been there—watching?

"Damien..." Elissa hurried from the dining room to meet him at the foot of the stairs. "What is this?"

She tried to take his bag, but he shook his head. "I can get it."

"But what are you doing with your luggage?"

He half grinned at the redhead. "You might say I had an epiphany of sorts after dinner—and it came to me that I should leave."

Lucy joined them, looking sad. "Must you?" It was strange how both Elissa and Lucy had gone along with Helen's ploy last night, but now, they looked as though they regretted it. "Are you sure you're up to it?"

He shrugged and chuckled without humor. "I'm not sure of anything—except that I need to go."

Lucy and Elissa turned toward Helen, their expressions telegraphed different messages. Lucy's stare pleaded that she *do* something, make him reconsider. Elissa's eyes were expressing how sorry she was, for she knew her baby sister's heart would suffer once he was gone.

When Helen only stood there, saying nothing, Damien seemed to take the hint and headed toward the door.

"But—but..." Lucy followed at his heels. "How will you—"

"I called our favorite cabby. He's here."

Elissa opened the door and both sisters tagged after him when he limped outside. The door didn't fully close.

Helen stood rooted beside the table, biting her lip. It

was better this way, she told herself. Better that she not see him off. She closed her eyes and bowed her head. The pain of knowing she would never see him again was hard to bear, and she was struck with such a sick, fiery gnawing she could hardly keep from crumbling to the floor. She so wanted to say goodbye, at least. To look into his face one last time. To wish him luck.

Long seconds ticked by, the air around her seething with wretched indecision. Bile rose in her throat and she clutched at her churning stomach. She felt ill, faint, feverish. What should she do? *What was best for him?*

The sound of a car trunk banging shut shot her through with panic. He was leaving! Now! Without thought, she followed her heart and rushed to the entrance just as he was kissing Elissa's cheek. "As I said before, Jack's a lucky guy. I envy his relationship with the Crosby sisters." He smiled at the redhead and turned to Lucy, who had tears in her eyes. He shook his head at her, brushing her cheek with his lips. "And I envy Stadler's luck. He doesn't deserve you."

Helen didn't expect it, didn't even know her arrival had been noticed. But he turned toward her as she stood there, paralyzed, clutching the door. His expression grew wry. "Helen?" He inclined his head. "Hear that?"

Confused by his cryptic question, she frowned, listening. But she heard nothing except distant highway traffic mingling with a low rustle of dry leaves in the breeze. "What?"

An eyebrow quirked and he grinned his crooked grin that always melted her insides. "It's the sound of the lid coming off my box."

His gentle teasing was too much for her heart to stand, too compelling to ignore, and she ran down the steps, grabbing his free hand in both of hers. "Damien, take care of yourself."

He squeezed her fingers. "I bet you say that to all the junk birds."

She smiled weakly, cherishing the feel of his long, callused fingers entwined with hers.

"You know, Helen, I never told you my nickname for you." Her throat closed and her stomach twisted as she anticipated the worst. "It's *bête noir*, and it means pet—" he stopped, his grin warm, teasing as he finished "—peeve. You've been a continuous personal vexation to me." He bent closer, whispering only for her to hear. "Thank you."

She stood, stunned, too close to him not to be affected by his potent nearness. She couldn't speak, didn't know what she would have said if she did. Even his nickname for her spoke volumes about the differences between them. *Bête noir*. French. He was so sophisticated, worldly, multilingual. And she? A simple girl who'd never been out of the Midwest, uneducated, shy. It was best that he was going, that she would never see him again.

His expression sobered, as though he could no longer carry out his charade of nonchalance. "You won't really marry Hirk, will you?"

Pain pinched her heart, and she knew the haunted look in his gaze would bedevil her all her life if she allowed the lie to continue. She shook her head.

He inhaled, appearing slightly mollified. "But you do think I'm a loser?"

The bleakness of his question was hard to take. Her breasts rose and fell with difficulty at each breath. How could she face her own lightless future knowing she'd hurt him any more than she had to? Swallowing, she disciplined her voice, whispering, "Only—only if you choose to be."

The relief that flitted across his features was profound. For a long moment he said nothing, watching her as if he were photographing her in his mind. "You're a royal pain, you know," he finally murmured.

Slipping his hand from hers, he cupped his fingers around her nape, the touch excruciating in its tenderness. With his thumb beneath her chin, he tilted her face. "They say you forget pain once it's gone." He lowered his face, brushing her lips with his. Then, almost as though he couldn't stop himself, his mouth closed over hers again, this time lingering, tasting her fully.

Sensations she hadn't thought she would ever experience tingled and danced through her, burning the miraculous event into her being for all eternity. *Damien was kissing her, really kissing her, the way a man kissed a woman.* Though it was goodbye, she knew she would hold the memory dear—forever.

When he finally lifted his mouth from hers, his gaze shimmered with soft emotion. "But I don't think I'll forget you."

The cab's departing dust had settled before she could move.

Damien left them on October 28. It was odd how the months began to melt into one another. November, December. Then January of a brand-new year.

The inn was thriving, and life was busy for the Crosby sisters. Though Helen was trying to forget Damien, there was a marriage on the first day of February that brought memories flooding back.

Hirk and Jule tied the knot in the inn's parlor that afternoon after he got back from his butter and egg route.

Hirk proudly showed off his new teeth, and Helen was astonished at how it transformed his face. He was really not a bad-looking man, at all.

Helen was happy for the couple, but melancholy dampened the experience, for she couldn't help but think about Damien—about her lost dreams of a life with him. No matter that he was gone and that she'd been the one to send him away, he was a part of her, and would always live in her heart.

He'd written a couple of times. Not long letters. Just asking how the Crosby girls were. Telling them he was "getting along fine" but revealing no real news about what he was doing. He did say he'd visited his parents in France and was heading back to the States. That had been a month ago. They hadn't heard from him since, but Helen didn't blame him for that. She hadn't answered either letter. It was just too hard.

That evening after the Boggs wedding, there was an earthquake in California. Thankfully it was centered in a less populated area, but the damage to property was great. A TV had been added to the parlor during the Christmas holidays, at the request of their guests. So it had become an evening ritual to gather around the set after dinner. Tonight, because of the quake, they were tuned to CNN.

Helen sat on the sofa with Thalia in her lap and little Love snuggled by her side. Honor and Cherish had gone to live with Bella, who'd renamed them Fritters and Fudge, two of her late husband's favorite foods.

"Oh my—heavens!" Lucy cried, drawing Helen's attention away from Love as he stretched out a paw to awaken Thalia in a bid to play chase-and-tumble.

"What is it?" Helen asked, and Lucy could only point at the TV, her expression stunned. Helen looked at the screen and her heart flew to her throat. "Damien!" she breathed aloud.

There he was. Microphone in hand, he picked his way through the rubble of what had once been a car lot. Though he was still using his cane, his gait seemed stronger, more sure.

Behind him, around him, cars were upended and strewn on their sides, many half buried in the earth. Damien reached a shiny, red Jaguar, its front bumper pointed skyward. He leaned against the sports car as though it were a monument to Nature's Fearful Superiority, the rich sound of his voice filling her heart with bittersweet memories.

He wore tan trousers and a knit shirt that emphasized his muscular physique. His hair was a little long, just as she remembered it, brushing his collar and falling across his eyepatch.

During a close-up shot, the camera captured the merciless damage to his face. The red scars on his cheek were still quite evident, yet seemed to give him a compelling male aura. It was ironic, that he somehow exuded an even more commanding presence, disfigured, than he had before his misfortune.

In that rugged, ruined landscape, this man, who'd obviously been through so much pain, himself, seemed natural, almost essential. As though on some gut level his very presence was assuring his viewers that, even amid disaster, there was hope.

Helen sat forward, absorbing him into every cell of her body, not really listening to what he was saying, for her heart pounded so hard she could hear nothing but the rush of her heated blood.

"He's made it!" Lucy cried, jumping up. "Elissa, come look! Damien's on TV!" She ran from the room to give her older sister the good news. *He had actually done it. All on his own, he'd fought his way back into the world he loved.*

As her cats leaped from the couch, Thalia taking up Love's playful challenge, Helen felt a tear tremble on her lower lashes. Her prayers for the man she loved had been answered. In her happiness for him, she focused on his provocative face, trying to ignore the hollow ache in her chest.

CHAPTER ELEVEN

APRIL began beautifully, with daffodils popping up all over the inn's yard and the budding of bright leaves on the trees. The sunshine was warm and welcome, and the inn continued to thrive, constantly filled to capacity.

The latest *Newsweek* came, and Helen's heart was pummeled with the reminder that Damien was most definitely back on the In List. Not that she was upset, just lonely for him and for the days they'd spent together that could never be again. That same morning cruel fate struck a second time. She spilled a cup of coffee all over herself when she saw a *People* magazine one of the guests left behind. Damien's face was emblazoned on the cover, proclaiming him America's Sexiest Man.

His eyepatch gave him a dashing, romantic image that apparently no woman in America was immune to. Helen was certainly no exception. Against her better judgment, she kept the magazine, hating herself for her weakness where the unattainable Mr. Lord was concerned.

In an attempt to safeguard her heart, Helen avoided watching his news segments on CNN. But evidently she was the only woman in the world to do so, considering his meteoric rise in popularity.

Lucy and Elissa watched the news station whenever they had time, squealing and shouting for Helen to come and see, every time he appeared doing special reports from around the country. But Helen didn't come. Didn't dare. She had to start breaking his hold on her heart some way. Had to get on with her life—a life without him. And running in to watch every time his face appeared on the TV screen was not the way to forget the man she loved and could never have.

The first week of April was over and Monday of the second week had been long and busy. Tired to the bone, Helen plodded through the staircase hall, heading for her room in the basement.

"Helen, ma'am?"

She turned, perplexed by the anemic tone in Jule's voice. The house maid looked competent and neat in her blue uniform, but her face had a greenish tinge. "Anything wrong?"

Jule groaned and put a trembly hand to her forehead. "I'm feelin' a little peaked." She leaned against the reception desk letting her broom clatter to the floor.

"You don't look well." Taking the woman's brawny arm, Helen led her into the parlor. Tonight, for a change, only a few guests had gathered after dinner and were playing bridge at a card table in the far corner. "Cola's good for an upset stomach. Would you like some, Jule?"

"I'd be real grateful, ma'am." She lowered herself gingerly into an overstuffed chair near the door. "Real grateful." It came out in a frail sigh.

A minute later, Helen rushed back into the room and gave Jule the glass. "Drink slowly. See if your stomach can take anything."

Jule nodded, sipping. "I'll be fine in a minute. Just—just sick and dizzy."

Helen peered at her inquisitively. "Sick and *dizzy*?"

Jule drank more. "Nothing real serious. Only a baby on the way." She smiled, blushing at Helen's gasp of surprise. Then she giggled. "I never been sick a day, and now I'm barfing in the mornings. Hirk's a real mental case."

Helen visualized Hirk as a nervous soon-to-be-father and smiled. "I'm happy for you both."

The house maid finished her cola, and sighed, resting back in the chair. "That sure did help." She straightened her glasses. "Thanks, ma'am."

Helen took the empty tumbler from her. "When's the baby due?"

"Early November. Hirk's so excited, he can't hardly remember his route these days. Delivered twelve pounds of butter to the widow Plunket's house, yesterday. Poor old thing didn't have room in her icebox for it all. Called him all cryin' and confused." Jule laughed, sounding better.

Elissa breezed in, going straight to the TV. "What? Nobody's watching television?" She flicked on the set. "Anybody mind if I turn it to CNN?"

Nobody seemed to care; the four guests involved in the bridge game nodded or didn't respond at all.

"Could I have another glass of cola?" Jule asked.

Helen jumped, then flushed, embarrassed that she'd allowed her mind to dwell for even a few seconds on the possibility that Damien's face might appear on the screen. She forced a smile. "Coming right up."

When she returned, Lucy had joined her sister on the sofa. "Oh, Helen…" Lucy popped up and dashed over, taking her younger sister's hand. "Come see."

Helen didn't realize Lucy's grip could be so viselike. But she clearly didn't intend to let go. "Look. There's Damien."

"Shush." Elissa looked around. "Where's that remote. I can't hear."

Helen sank down on the sofa cushions, her knees too mushy to do anything else. *He* was there, on the screen. And just as she feared, she couldn't turn away. His hair was charmingly windswept as he stood on a sandy rise before a churning sea.

"What is it?" Lucy asked. "Did that tropical storm turn back toward Florida?"

"I don't know. I can't hear." Elissa jumped up. "There's that darned remote." She hurried to the end table beside the leather chair and grabbed it.

"Uh—" Helen broke in. "I really have a lot of things to—"

"Hush! Don't you want to hear about the tropical storm?" Elissa came back and sat down, eyeing the screen.

"I doubt that Branson's in imminent danger," Helen muttered.

"I wonder if Damien is?" Lucy patted her sister's hand, but continued to face the TV. "He looks wonderful. You must be proud of your part in his recovery."

Helen sucked in a breath as the sound came up and they could hear Damien's voice. "Since the danger is past, I'm taking this opportunity to announce that I've been reassigned to CNN's Baltic news bureau."

Lucy clasped her hands before her. "Oh, how wonderful for him!"

"He's getting everything he wanted." Elissa twisted to face Helen, then her smile faded slightly. "Oh, honey. You did a wonderful thing for him. Try to think of it like that."

"But I won't be going to the Baltic," he went on.

All three sisters froze in surprise, staring at the screen.

"Because my first novel will be coming out in a few months, and I'm working on a new book. Also, I've accepted a position with the *New York Times* to write a political column. So this will be my last report for CNN."

Helen was stunned. "His first novel?" She hugged herself, for she was suddenly shivering. "I knew it was good!"

"But before I sign off, I have something personal to say to a woman I owe a great deal to." He paused, his expression charmingly earnest. "I hope you're listening, Helen."

"*Helen*, ma'am!" Jule blurted out, leaping up. "Is Mr. Lord talkin' to you?"

The entire room went still, the bridge game forgotten. Everyone was staring her way.

She gulped, wondering how many Helens he knew. Probably a thousand, since his newfound popularity. She couldn't be *the* Helen. Why would he have something to say to her? He hadn't seen her in almost six months.

The camera moved in for a close-up of the dark gaze she remembered fondly in her heart, and that same wonderful smile he had used so sparingly while at the inn. But the smile was somehow different this time, more gentle, loving and vulnerable. "Helen," he spoke the name softly, and it seemed as though he were looking directly at her. "I've decided I believe in myths. Will you marry me?"

No one in the parlor made a sound. Even the news anchor gaped, speechless, as the credits rolled. She found herself standing, staring at the screen as a commercial for toothpaste came on. Had she really seen that, or was her foolish mind playing tricks? "What—what did he say?" Her voice was shaky.

"I said I believe in myths," a deep voice replied.

She spun to see a tall man silhouetted in the parlor entrance. Before she could absorb what was happening, he began to walk toward her. This man, who bore a cruel resemblance to Damien, used no cane.

"And I asked you to marry me," he murmured.

"Oh my..." Lucy said through a sigh.

"Wow." Elissa stood and touched Helen on the arm. "Are you okay?"

When Helen managed a nod, Elissa gave her a light shove. "Then go, girl. Answer the man."

She'd only moved two faltering steps forward when he reached her, taking her hands in his. "Hi." He gazed down at her, and she couldn't help but be affected by the thoroughly masculine appeal of his smile. "Did anybody ever tell you you're a lousy letter writer?"

Her heart thudded like a drum, and she could hardly get her brain to function. Her throat dry and scratchy, she said, "But, I never sent you any letters."

He chuckled, bending to brush her lips with a kiss. "Exactly." When he lifted his head, he indicated Elissa. "Luckily your sister was better at it. She kept me informed about how you were doing, since for some reason I couldn't seem to break contact with my little *bête noir*." She swallowed. His fingers holding hers were beautiful torture. "So I asked her to make sure you watched CNN tonight."

She blinked at the news of a conspiracy between her sisters and Damien, but couldn't respond.

"Helen," he repeated, his expression going concerned. "Can you hear me?"

He squeezed her hands, bringing her partly out of her stupor. "I—I thought marriage wasn't in your plans."

He shook his head ruefully. "I was a damned fool for a lot of years." Releasing her fingers he took her face between his big, warm hands. "I didn't plan to. I missed you every day after I left. I fought it like hell. But when I was given that foreign assignment, I knew I had to turn it down. My book had sold, just as you thought it would.

I only sent it in because of you, by the way." He stroked her lower lip with his thumb. "When I realized I'd be leaving the country—doing what I'd thought I *had* to do to be happy—all I could think about was how far away I'd be from you. And I was miserable."

Unable to stop herself, she kissed the thumb that was stroking her lip, and his expression brightened. "I love you, Helen. I learned when a man is miserable without a woman, then marriage becomes an option. I just never knew how love felt until you came into my life." He chuckled reflectively. "As I said, I was a damn fool for a lot of years."

She was in awe of what he was telling her. These were the words she'd longed for him to say. But she'd given up hope of ever hearing them. A thousand times she'd given up, on long, lonely nights when her tears stained her pillow. "Damien..." His name came out like a lament, and his brow furrowed.

"Helen, don't say no." He pulled her into his arms and held her close. She could feel the jolt of his rapid heartbeats against her breasts, and knew how deeply he was moved by her nearness. "Sweetheart, I want us to buy a house in upstate New York big enough for six kids, a dozen orphaned kittens, a three-legged mutt and maybe a needy sparrow now and then. How does that sound to you?"

His scent, his closeness, were mesmerizing, but not as mesmerizing as his soft vow of love and commitment. She couldn't believe it. Couldn't grasp the magnitude of it. Grabbing his shirtfront in wads, she fought to make sense of it all. "This can't be real! How can you really be here?"

"The miracle of tape, darling. Now answer my question."

Overwhelmed by such happiness she feared she might burst with it, she drew up on tiptoe and kissed his jaw. "Oh, Damien, you could live in the top of a tree and insist you wanted to raise poisonous spiders, and I'd be *thrilled* to live up there with you."

His chuckle was a rich, satiny rumble of sound, and she relished the feel of it all the way to her toes. "That's what I needed to hear—kid."

A sob of joy burst from her throat, but she angled her face away from his to peer at his teasing grin. "Don't call me kid."

He winked. "Whatever you say, pumpkin pie. If you promise not to take back your 'yes' once I give you the bad news."

Even his dire warning didn't dull her happiness, but she tilted her head, curious. "What bad news?"

He bent to whisper in her ear so that only she could hear. "My mother was a twin. You may have six babies more quickly than you want."

Her heart tumbled over itself from pure hunger for this man, who seemed to be perfectly willing to father three sets of twins with her. When she met his gaze, her eyes brimmed with blissful tears. "If that's the worst news you can give me, I'm going to be a very happy woman."

He kissed away a tear that had escaped to her cheek, his face so full of erotic promise, she could hardly keep from sinking to the floor in a puddle of desire. "I heard somewhere you prefer April weddings," he whispered against her lips.

She was startled by his remark, then remembered she'd said that to Hirk at dinner the night before Damien had gone away. *He'd remembered.* How sweet. "Since it's April now..." She nuzzled his throat. "I admit, it's my *very* favorite month for a wedding."

"We'll have to see what we can do about that." He nipped her earlobe, then trailed tickling, tempting kisses across to her mouth for one brief taste. "I think we should continue this in private," he whispered.

The scorching intent in his gaze made her body sing with womanly anticipation, and she nodded. "We have so much to—talk about."

"Right." He winked at her, looking even more stunningly virile than she remembered. Something undeniable surged between them, of love given and shared forever. In one swift motion, she was lifted into his arms.

Amid squeals from her sisters and *oohs* and *ahs* from their guests, he carried her from the room.

A few days later, they were married, and Helen proved to her new husband exactly how much of a grown-up woman she had become. While Damien, no longer a stranger to himself, passionately confirmed his belief that she was the most beautiful woman on earth.

The D'Amour myth had worked its magic.

*   *   *   *   *

Renee Roszel's ENCHANTED BRIDES
trilogy continues with Lucy's Story.
Look out for this in early 1998.

EVER HAD ONE OF THOSE DAYS?

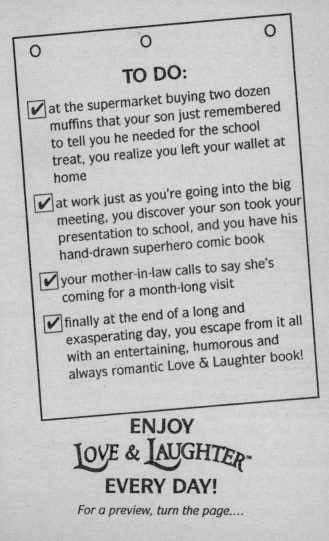

TO DO:

☑ at the supermarket buying two dozen muffins that your son just remembered to tell you he needed for the school treat, you realize you left your wallet at home

☑ at work just as you're going into the big meeting, you discover your son took your presentation to school, and you have his hand-drawn superhero comic book

☑ your mother-in-law calls to say she's coming for a month-long visit

☑ finally at the end of a long and exasperating day, you escape from it all with an entertaining, humorous and always romantic Love & Laughter book!

ENJOY
LOVE & LAUGHTER™
EVERY DAY!

For a preview, turn the page....

———————

"YOU'RE A VERY popular lady," Jed Kelley observed as Augustina closed the door on her suitors.

She waved a hand. "Just two of a dozen." Technically true since her grandmother had put her on the open market. "You're not afraid of a little competition, are you?"

"Competition?" He looked puzzled. "I thought the position was mine."

Augustina shook her head, smiling coyly. "You didn't think Grandmother was the final arbiter of the decision, did you? I say a trial period is in order." No matter that Jed Kelley had miraculously passed Grandmother's muster, Augustina felt the need for a little propriety. But, on the other hand, she could be married before the summer was out and be free as a bird, with the added bonus of a husband it wouldn't be all that difficult to learn to love.

She got up the courage to reach for his hand, and then just like that, she—Miss Gussy Gutless Fairchild—was holding Jed Kelley's hand. He looked down at their linked hands. "Of course, you don't really know what sort of work I can do, do you?"

A funny way to put it, she thought absently, cradling his callused hand between both of her own. "We can get to know each other, and then, if that works out…'' she murmured. *Wow*. If she'd known what this arranged marriage thing was all about, she'd have been a supporter of Grandmother's campaign from the start!

''Are you a palm reader?'' Jed asked gruffly. His voice was as raspy as sandpaper and it was rubbing her all the right ways, but the question flustered her. She dropped his hand.

''I'm sorry.''

''No problem,'' he said, ''as long as I'm hired.''

''Hired!'' she scoffed. ''What a way of putting it!''

Jed folded his arms across his chest. ''So we're back to the trial period.''

''Yes.'' Augustina frowned and her gaze dropped to his work boots. Okay, so he wasn't as well off as the majority of her suitors, but really, did he think she was going to *pay* him to marry her?

''Fine, then.'' He flipped her a wave and, speechless, she watched him leave. She was trembling all over like a malaria victim in a snowstorm, shot with hot charges and cold shivers until her brain was numb. This couldn't be true. Fantasy men didn't happen to nice girls like her.

''Augustina?''

Her grandmother's voice intruded on Gussy's privacy. ''Ahh. There you are. I see you met the new gardener?''

Take 4 bestselling love stories FREE

Plus get a FREE surprise gift!

HARLEQUIN WOMEN KNOW ROMANCE WHEN THEY SEE IT.

And they'll see it on **ROMANCE CLASSICS**, the new 24-hour TV channel devoted to romantic movies and original programs like the special **Romantically Speaking-Harlequin® Goes Prime Time.**

Romantically Speaking-Harlequin® Goes Prime Time introduces you to many of your favorite romance authors in a program developed exclusively for Harlequin® readers.

Watch for **Romantically Speaking-Harlequin® Goes Prime Time** beginning in the summer of 1997.

If you're not receiving ROMANCE CLASSICS, call your local cable operator or satellite provider and ask for it today!

Escape to the network of your dreams.

Free Gift Offer

With a Free Gift proof-of-purchase
from any Harlequin® book, you can receive
a beautiful cubic zirconia pendant.

This stunning marquise-shaped stone is a genuine cubic
zirconia—accented by an 18" gold tone necklace.
(Approximate retail value $19.95)

Send for yours today...
compliments of

To receive your free gift, a cubic zirconia pendant, send us one original proof-of-purchase, photocopies not accepted, from the back of any Harlequin Romance®, Harlequin Presents®, Harlequin Temptation®, Harlequin Superromance®, Harlequin Intrigue®, Harlequin American Romance®, or Harlequin Historicals® title available at your favorite retail outlet, together with the Free Gift Certificate, plus a check or money order for $1.65 U.S./$2.15 CAN. (do not send cash) to cover postage and handling, payable to Harlequin Free Gift Offer. We will send you the specified gift. Allow 6 to 8 weeks for delivery. Offer good until December 31, 1997, or while quantities last. Offer valid in the U.S. and Canada only.

Free Gift Certificate

Name: _____

Address: _____

City: _____ State/Province: _____ Zip/Postal Code: _____

Mail this certificate, one proof-of-purchase and a check or money order for postage and handling to: HARLEQUIN FREE GIFT OFFER 1997. In the U.S.: 3010 Walden Avenue, P.O. Box 9071, Buffalo NY 14269-9057. In Canada: P.O. Box 604, Fort Erie, Ontario L2Z 5X3.

FREE GIFT OFFER   084-KEZ
ONE PROOF-OF-PURCHASE
To collect your fabulous FREE GIFT, a cubic zirconia pendant, you must include this original proof-of-purchase for each gift with the properly completed Free Gift Certificate.

084-KEZR